Four Years Is A Long Time

Sean's eyes pierced Blair, willing her to feel again. A trembling awareness of him was awakened within her, and she was angry at herself for reacting in such a way.

Blair took a deep, shuddering breath. "This was a mistake. I knew better than to accept this job. I'm sorry, Sean, I want nothing more than to work, but I don't date. I'm just not ready for any involvements."

Sean shook his head fiercely. "Don't lie to me...or to yourself. I need you, so I'll wait, but only for a little while."

One burning thought burst into Blair's mind. Knowing how Sean affected her, how could she work with him and still remain faithful to her husband's memory?

Dear Reader:

Romance offers us all so much. It makes us "walk on sunshine." It gives us hope. It takes us out of our own lives, encouraging us to reach out to others. Janet Dailey is fond of saying that romance is a state of mind, that it could happen anywhere. Yet nowhere does romance seem to be as good as when it happens *here*.

Starting in February 1986, Silhouette Special Edition will feature the AMERICAN TRIBUTE—a tribute to America, where romance has never been so wonderful. For six consecutive months, one out of every six Special Editions will be an episode in the AMERICAN TRIBUTE, a portrait of the lives of six women, all from Oklahoma. Look for the first book, *Love's Haunting Refrain* by Ada Steward, as well as stories by other favorites—Jeanne Stephens, Gena Dalton, Elaine Camp and Renee Roszel. You'll know the AMERICAN TRIBUTE by its patriotic stripe under the Silhouette Special Edition border.

AMERICAN TRIBUTE—six women, six stories, starting in February.

AMERICAN TRIBUTE—one of the reasons Silhouette Special Edition is just that—Special.

The Editors at Silhouette Books

MONICA BARRIE
Ashes of the Past

Silhouette Special Edition

Published by Silhouette Books New York

America's Publisher of Contemporary Romance

By its very nature,
this novel can only be dedicated
to the following three people:

My researcher, Leslie;
My editor, (the one with the four first names) Mary Clare;
And without a doubt, my agent, Julia.

SILHOUETTE BOOKS
300 E. 42nd St., New York, N.Y. 10017

ISBN: 0-373-09279-2

First Silhouette Books printing December 1985

10 9 8 7 6 5 4 3 2 1

MONICA BARRIE,

a native of New York State, has traveled extensively around the world but has returned to settle in New York. A prolific romance writer, Monica's tightly woven emotional stories are drawn from her inherent understanding of relationships between men and women.

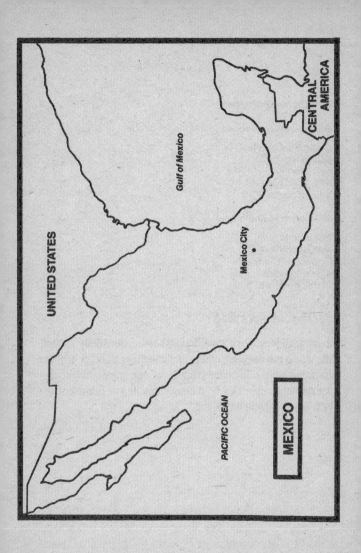

Chapter One

The hum of conversation and the music grew loud when the bedroom door opened. Turning, Blair Sanders saw Alice Daniels step inside and close the door behind her.

"Why are you hiding in here?" Alice asked.

Blair shrugged her bare and shapely shoulders. "I'm not hiding, just taking a breather," she said.

"You're supposed to be out there meeting people and having fun."

"I've met a lot of them already," Blair replied, shaking her head at the same time. "Two men have already asked me out, or at least I think that's what they did. Both gave me their cards and told me to call if I was interested." Blair sighed longingly. "Things have really changed in the past few years."

"Not really," Alice replied. "And you can't blame them. I mean you do look absolutely gorgeous in that dress. It really is a great dress."

Blair shook her head again. "I would hope you like it; you are the one who picked it out for me."

"I do have good taste, don't I?" Alice asked.

"In clothing perhaps..." Blair said with a warm smile.

"In a lot of things. Come back to the party with me," Alice half ordered, taking Blair's arm and leading her from the security and sanctity of the bedroom.

The moment Blair was able to free herself from Alice's clutches, she went over to a large picture window and gazed down at the night lights of Manhattan in a futile effort to will herself to participate in the party.

It was a lively party that was taking place in the tastefully decorated apartment, filled with a multitude of people, most of whom were smiling and enjoying—or seeming to enjoy—themselves. If there were any who were not having a good time, they managed to mask their emotions in a way that Blair would have liked to.

It wasn't that she disliked parties; at one time in her life she had enjoyed them: she never went to parties any more—at least not in the past four years. But tonight was different, and she had come to this gathering, hosted by her closest friend, Alice Daniels, at Alice's insistence. "Business," Alice had told her, "it's for business."

Besides being her best friend, Alice Daniels was a literary agent of the highest repute. This party was attended by a number of well-known authors, editors and agents; most of whom she had been forced to meet during the past hour and a half because it would benefit her to do so. Yet it was not the sort of party Blair would have chosen to attend.

No party was. *Not since Brian,* she told herself silently. But she was here for business, and she accepted that fact. Not to do business, but to meet the various people she was currently doing work for and those she had done work for in the past.

Although Blair preferred the anonymity of dealing with her clients via the mail and telephone rather than venturing into the public, she had known when Alice had cajoled her into attending the party that Alice was right. It would be good for her to meet the people she did research for and to let them know it was a real flesh-and-blood person who discovered their information and made their lives easier by doing so.

Behind her, the voices in the room faded as Blair thought back to the times before she had started her own business. She thought of the good times, and of the saddest time of all. But before her mind became entrenched within the past, she became aware of a couple who had moved next to her.

Blair glanced at the couple. The woman was statuesque, elegant, and blonde; her shoulder-length hair shimmered in the apartment's light, and the perfection of her features seemed as if they'd come straight from the cover of *Vogue.*

Suddenly, Blair found herself looking directly into the man's eyes, her entire being focused intently on him. And the man, Blair realized, was none other than Sean Mathias, the best-selling author. He was one of the few authors she had not yet been introduced to tonight. He was also an author she had done research for several times in the past.

Blair pulled her eyes from his and looked out the window. But a few moments later, and without being obvious, Blair was again studying the man. His dark and handsome good looks lent credence to all the things she'd ever heard of him—that, and the beautiful blonde who was hanging on to his every word.

Forcefully, and not knowing why she was so drawn to him, Blair looked out at Manhattan without seeing its myriad glittering lights. All she saw was the couples' reflection clearly etched on the window's surface. Because of their closeness she could not help overhearing their conversation, the very content of which caught her interest immediately.

"I think it will sell, and I intend to write it," Sean said.

"I don't know.... I mean, reincarnation?" questioned the blonde.

"Reincarnation fascinates everyone. The possibility of living multiple lives, and especially of loving someone time and time again, is something that everyone would like to read about, whether they believe in it or not," Sean stated.

"You're a novelist, Sean. Your milieu is fiction. Wouldn't you do better setting the book up as a novel?" the woman asked.

"Not this time, Joyce," Sean stated adamantly. His deep brown eyes hardened for an instant; the shapely blonde merely shrugged her shoulders. "Wouldn't you like to know if you had once been living in the time of say...Caesar?"

Before the woman had a chance to answer, Blair, still watching their reflections in the window, belatedly realized that Sean Mathias's gaze was now fixed on her. Blair pretended not to notice him.

"And you? What do you believe in?" the author asked, stepping closer to Blair. His companion seemed to be appraising her while Sean spoke.

Blair stared at him in shock. She had been unprepared for his direct question. Looking into his handsome face, she willed her voice to work.

"Myself," she said, responding to his question with a sureness she did not feel.

"Do you think that love can survive eternity?"

"I think that love has to," Blair replied, as she tried to control the way her heart raced under the assault of his eyes.

"Many people do. In part, that's a basis for one reincarnation theory."

Blair shook her head slowly. "I know very little about reincarnation."

"What do you know about?" Sean asked, his eyes sweeping boldly across her features.

Blair didn't respond immediately; rather she met his gaze with her own. "I know what I need to, to survive in this lifetime," Blair said in a level voice. "Good evening," she added. With that, Blair turned and walked across the room.

Although she walked steadily, she felt anything but steady. The moment he'd spoken to her, she had felt a strange reaction: her stomach had tightened, and her breathing had grown shallow.

The way his deep brown gaze had fastened onto hers and the resonant timbre of his voice had affected her swiftly. She had sensed the importance of getting away from him, and had done so as quickly as possible. Yet even as she walked across the crowded room, she could feel his eyes following her.

I shouldn't have come, Blair told herself, angry that the man had been able to pierce the shell she wore about herself.

Blair negotiated her way across the room until she spotted Alice Daniels. Catching Alice's eye, she signaled with a nod of her head. A moment later, Alice came over to her.

"Enjoying yourself?"

"I think I'm going to call it a night," Blair said.

Alice's face reflected disappointment. "It's early," Alice argued.

"For you. I have work to do tomorrow."

"You hate it!"

"I don't hate the party, Alice, it's just not my cup of tea. You know that."

"You need to venture into the real world occasionally to find out what your cup of tea is," Alice stated, her voice tinged with regret.

Blair shook her head slowly. "When I'm ready, Alice, I will, I promise."

"All right," Alice said in defeat. "I'll call you tomorrow."

The party had dwindled down to only a few people, and as Alice Daniels stood near the door bidding her guests good-night, Sean approached her.

"What did Joyce think about the reincarnation theme?" Alice asked Sean. Joyce Leonard was the editor of Sean's last three novels, all best-sellers.

"She thought it would be better as a novel," he told her.

"She doesn't really have any choice. The wording on the option clause is very clear. Their option is on your next work, it doesn't differentiate between fiction and nonfiction. She knows that if she turns it down, there are a dozen other publishers who'll snap it up just to get the next Sean Mathias book."

"I know, but Joyce is the best editor I've ever worked with. I want to stay with her."

"You will, I'll take care of everything," Alice promised.

"Good," he said, knowing that Alice had never let him down. "There is one other thing you could take care of now," Sean said, his eyes locking on Alice's.

"Yes?" Alice was used to her clients' requests, and none had ever surprised her, but the sudden glint in Sean's eyes underscored a warning within them.

"There was a woman here before...I'd like to know who she is."

"There were thirty women here," Alice told him dryly.

"This one kept to herself. She was wearing a strapless beige dress. She has incredibly beautiful features and was about five four or so, with shortish, curly hair that showed off her—"

"Forget it," Alice stated, cutting him off because she had immediately known whom he meant.

Sean smiled, continuing as if Alice hadn't spoken. "That showed off her lovely face and beautiful eyes. *I want to see her again.*"

"Sean, trust me, she isn't for you."

"Who is she for?"

Alice exhaled slowly. "No one right now. Besides, you can't get involved with her. You don't want to mix business with pleasure."

"What are you talking about?"

"The lady in question is Blair Sanders. She's done...her company has done the research for your last two novels."

"Sanders Research," Sean said with a nod. "Alice, I want to see her again. I... It's important to me." As he spoke, Sean realized just how true his words were.

Alice stared at him for a moment, torn between her loyalty to her friend and what she was so suddenly reading in Sean's face.

"I don't know if that's possible," she said in a low voice.

"You know better than that, Alice. Anything is possible."

Alice closed her eyes for a moment, balancing her loyalty to her friend against her loyalty to her author, who was also her friend. And then she thought about Blair and everything Blair had been through. "It's a long story, Sean."

"I have the time."

"Okay," she whispered, looking around the room. "We'll talk when everyone is gone."

Blair unlocked the door and let herself into her apartment. She was tired, but not ready for sleep. After changing from her dress into her robe, she went into the living room and sat down on the couch.

Her thoughts were troubled, and she could not calm herself. She knew that Sean Mathias, and her unwarranted reaction to him, were a part of the reason for this.

Blair shook her head in an effort to clear her mind of the party and of Sean Mathias. But the disturbing image of the handsome writer refused to leave her mind's eye.

Why did I act like such a fool, she wondered, thinking back to her haughty reaction to the writer's questions. Blair had felt that she didn't belong with the other guests at the party; she hadn't felt that she belonged in any group of people for a long time.

Closing her eyes, Blair again tried to push away the dark mood that had captured her. She understood that it wasn't a mood; rather, it was a state of mind that was so deeply a part of her that it was almost second nature, and had been for the past four years.

"Why did it have to happen?" she asked aloud. Opening her eyes, she looked at the wedding portrait hanging on the wall across from her. The sparkling smile that had been on her face then was something she believed she would never feel again.

"Brian," she whispered to the tuxedo-clad man standing next to her in the photo. Suddenly, she was thinking about Sean Mathias's strange conversation with the blonde. *Was there really such a thing as reincarnation?*

"Will I find you again in another lifetime?" she asked the image of the man who had been her husband.

Tears fell from her eyes, but she did not feel them. All Blair felt was the heartrending pain that always accompanied her thoughts of Brian. "I miss you so much," she whispered.

Blair knew that life wasn't fair. She had learned that four years before, when Brian had been taken from her so soon after they were married. Sighing, Blair allowed herself to think back to that wonderful time five years before when she had met and married Brian. Blair had just come to New York, and had found work as a documentary researcher for WNTB-TV. On her first assignment she had met Brian, who had been an investigative reporter for the station.

Within three days they were seeing each other every chance they had. Two months later, and a week after her twenty-third birthday, they had gotten married. For a year their life had been perfect. The love they held for each other deepened with each day, while the bond that they shared grew stronger and stronger.

But a year almost to the day that they had wed, Brian had died in an automobile accident. Even in the terrible aftermath of her loss, Blair knew that the perfection of their strong yet gentle love would never again be duplicated.

It had taken Blair a year to come to terms with her loss—a year that had been filled with a thousand emotions ranging from utter despair to heartaching pain. Shortly after Brian's death, she had been overcome with anger and hate for Brian's deserting her and leaving her to face the world alone. But anger could only last so long. Then one morning she had awakened to reality and to the realization that she had to find a way to go on with her life; she had known it as certainly as she had known Brian would want her to.

Blair had decided to go back to work, but she could not face returning to the television station where so many memories were. Instead, she had called Alice

Daniels and invited her to lunch. That was the day Sanders Research had been born. With Alice's help— and her long list of clients—Blair began to do literary research for writers.

Her friend Alice had given her the idea by suggesting she combine her past experience with something that would be a challenge for her. And it was Alice, again, who had arranged for Blair to do research for her clients.

Within a twelve-month period, Blair had become extremely busy and had taken on two assistants. Over the next three years, the business had blossomed, and she had all the work she could handle.

Blair worked hard, sometimes spending twelve to sixteen hours a day doing her research. She didn't mind the hours; in fact, she looked forward to them, for in them she hid from the pain of her memories. But Blair knew that no matter how hard she tried to avoid thinking of anything other than work, there was some.hing lacking in her life.

Brian, she tolc herself silently. Again, Sean Mathias's words returned to her mind. She wondered what kind of book he was working on. As an author, Sean's novels were usually about the contemporary world, and were filled with adventure, excitement and romance. When a Sean Mathias novel was published, like a Sidney Sheldon, a Harold Robbins, or a Robert Ludlum novel, it was an instant best-seller. A Sean Mathias novel was a good read.

Standing, Blair took her gaze from the wedding portrait and went into her bedroom. She glanced at the clock and saw that it was nearly midnight. With a yawn Blair slipped between the covers and closed her eyes to await sleep.

A half hour later she was still awake, her thoughts mired in the past. Blair raised her left hand to look at the thin gold band on her ring finger. Her eyes misted again. She had never taken the ring off since Brian's death and always looked at it so that she would never forget who she was.

Not once in the past four years had Blair dated a man; all her energy was funneled into her work. Whenever someone called and asked her out she politely and firmly turned him down. Blair preferred to lead her life this way. She would never be unfaithful to Brian's memory.

Could there really be any truth to reincarnation, she wondered as Sean Mathias's words again intruded upon her. And slowly, without her realizing it, sleep eased Blair from her troubled thoughts.

When Blair arrived at her offices, she had succeeded in pushing all thoughts of the previous night away, and put herself fully into her work. She was compiling the results of the research that she and her staff had done for Thomas Mannering, the author she had done her first research job for.

She was so lost in thought that she did not hear her intercom, and a few minutes later Laura, her assistant, came into her office.

"Blair," Laura called.

Blair glanced up, a question on her face.

"Alice Daniels is on the phone."

"Why didn't you buzz me?" Blair asked.

"I did."

"Oh.... Thanks," she said as she lifted the receiver. "Hi."

"Hi. How are you today?" Alice asked.

"Fine," Blair said. "Alice, I'm sorry about running out. It just got to be too much for me."

"I understand," Alice told her. Blair knew her friend meant what she said.

"It was a lovely party."

"It was all right," Alice replied. "How about dinner tonight?"

"I'd love to, but I'm trying to finish Mannering's research," Blair explained.

"Tomorrow night? My treat?" Alice asked.

"Fine," Blair said.

"By the way, I'll also have some new work for you."

"Good. Anything interesting?"

Alice's laugh caught Blair off guard. "I think so," Alice said a moment later.

"What do you find so humorous?" Blair asked. In the background she could hear Alice's other phone begin to ring.

"It's just my mood," Alice told her. "See you tomorrow," she said quickly.

Shrugging her shoulders, Blair went back to work. But her own mood of total concentration on the job at hand had been shattered, and instead of seeing the neatly printed words that filled the report, she was again thinking about the possibilities of reincarnation and what it might mean to her.

The hubbub of the neighborhood eatery, Jason's, was a sound Blair had become used to over the years. And sitting in a rear booth, she felt at home. She had arrived at the restaurant at the same time as Alice, and since it was not yet the dinner hour, they'd been able to choose their own booth.

After ordering cocktails, Blair asked Alice about the new research job. Alice smiled. "It's intriguing."

"What's intriguing?" Blair asked, but had to wait while their drinks were served.

Alice lifted her glass in toast. "To a great challenge," Alice whispered.

Blair sipped her white wine, put down the glass and sat deeper into the cushions of the booth. She stared openly at Alice as she formed her question. "What sort of a great challenge?" Blair asked suspiciously.

Alice was silent, her expression one of amusement. "Well?" Blair prompted.

"One of my writers has some very important research to be done. He wants you to do it."

"That's not a challenge," Blair said.

"He wants you to do it personally, not give it to one of your assistants. It's researching reincarnation," Alice said.

Blair's hand tightened on the stem of the wineglass, her knuckles turned white, but she did not speak.

"Blair?"

"Why does Sean Mathias want me to do the work personally? I have a capable staff," she reminded Alice.

"How did you know it was Sean?" Alice asked in surprise.

"Perhaps I'm psychic!" Blair told her sarcastically.

"Then you're perfect for this job," Alice said smoothly. "Truthfully, Blair, Sean is sensitive to his work and sensitive to the people he works with. This book represents a very different direction for him. His literary credentials will be on the line. He...no, I need to make sure that everything is perfect for this book."

Although the previous day had been filled with thoughts of Sean Mathias and reincarnation, a tendril of doubt rose in response to Alice's plea. "Alice, I...I have another job I haven't finished yet." But that was just an excuse she used, because the job could be handled by either of her assistants.

Before Alice could speak, the waiter brought over the menus. When he was gone, Alice continued. "Please, Blair, it's very important—for more than the obvious reasons. Do it for me, just this once," Alice pleaded.

Blair shook her head but did not turn Alice down. Confused at her reactions, Blair picked up the menu and began to look it over. Yet she saw none of the selections as her mind worked furiously on Alice's request. All the while, she remembered the way Sean had looked at her and remembered, too, the passion she'd heard in his voice when he'd spoken of reincarnation. In that instant, Blair knew she wanted to learn more about reincarnation.

Blair lowered the menu to look at her friend. "Alice, I...I just don't know."

"Blair, please."

"All right," Blair finally whispered, ignoring the vision of Sean's deep eyes that floated hauntingly before her.

"Wonderful!" Alice declared. "What are you going to have for dinner?"

Blair shrugged. "A salad. I'm not very hungry."

A moment later the waiter reappeared. Blair ordered her salad, and Alice ordered Dover sole. While they waited for their food, Alice explained about Sean's new book and the risk he was taking in writing a nonfiction book, especially on a topic as touchy as reincarnation.

"But everyone really wants to know about it, even if they won't admit it," Alice added.

"Won't Mr. Mathias be labeled an occultist?" Blair asked.

"I hope not. Besides, it will only be one book. He already has his next novel outlined. And it's anything but occult!"

The food arrived then, and the women ate silently. When coffee was served, Alice smiled at Blair. "I really am glad you're going to do this research. If anyone can do it right, it's you," Alice stated, her voice growing excited as she spoke. "I'll send over directions to Sean's house. He expects you to arrive tomorrow afternoon. You can stay at his house if you want."

"What? Alice..." Blair protested, her face suddenly stiff and her mind reeling under the impact of Alice's words.

"Oh, did I forget to tell you that you'll have to work directly with Sean?" Alice asked innocently.

"No!" Blair snapped, slamming her cup down and ignoring the coffee that sloshed over the rim and onto her fingers.

"Blair..."

"You know my rules. I work by myself, not with a client. I tried that once and it doesn't work."

"Blair, I'm asking you to do this for me."

Blair paused, holding back her angry retort as she listened to the tone of her friend's voice and not the words Alice had spoken. She studied Alice's face for a moment before she finally replied in a low voice.

"Why, Alice? Why can't one of my assistants do it?"

"They probably could," Alice admitted. "But I *need* you to be the one. Everything has to be right on this, everything," Alice repeated.

"I don't like this at all."

"But you'll do it?"

Blair's eyes swept across Alice's pretty features. She knew her friend well and believed that if Alice was asking her for this favor, it was truly important to her. She was aware that she owed Alice a great deal for all that her friend had done for her, even though Alice had never once mentioned a debt. Blair sighed. "I'll do it...for you."

"Thanks, Blair," Alice said quickly.

"But not tomorrow. I have to clear up a few things. The day after, okay?"

"Okay," Alice said with a friendly sparkle in her eyes.

The next day, Blair worked at her fastest pace in an effort to clear up all the work that she had. By three o'clock she was finished, and at four a messenger arrived with the envelope from Alice. Inside was a map of New York state and typed directions to Sean Mathias's house, which was on the Pennsylvania side of the Delaware River. A rental-car reservation number was attached to the papers, and the car was reserved for noon, the next day.

What did I do? A favor for my friend, she said in answer to her question.

After assigning to her second assistant, Stephanie, the research project she had chosen to work on herself, she went over the accounts and balanced the books.

She got home shortly after eight o'clock and, after eating a light dinner, packed a suitcase with three days' worth of clothing. For the remainder of the night she did her best not to think of Sean Mathias or of the work she would be doing. By the time she fell asleep, a feeling she had not felt in a long time began to rise within her. It was a feeling of excitement, and with it was a desire to see what tomorrow would bring.

Once again, as she did every night, she lifted her left hand and gazed at the thin wedding band on her ring finger.

Chapter Two

The afternoon sun sent showers of color in rainbow arcs dancing across the rocks. At this point of the Delaware River where the white-water rapids flowed, civilization seemed much farther than a three-hour drive from Manhattan.

Blair took in the picturesque view while she looked for the large white house that was the landmark in her directions. A quarter of a mile past the house would be the small road that led to a wooden bridge spanning the river, the road that would take her from New York into Pennsylvania.

Blair was anxious about the day because it was only the second time since starting Sanders Research that she would be working directly with a client. Her usual routine was contact through phone calls or letters. Her first experience at doing research with an author had ended disastrously. He had been like a tyrannical boss standing over her at every moment. As a result, she had been unable to complete the research and had refused to do any further work for the man.

This is for Alice, she reminded herself, feeling no less trepidation than before.

A moment later she spotted the large white Victorian house and slowed the car. Exactly one quarter of a mile later, she reached the turn and maneuvered the car onto the narrow road. Glancing at her watch, Blair saw that it was almost three o'clock.

Again, apprehension tried to gain a handhold in her mind, but she refused to let it. Instead, she thought about the upcoming research and let the sense of excitement about it grow stronger.

A moment later the wooden bridge came into view. Crossing it, she made the first right turn as the directions stated. Five minutes later she reached a long and winding drive.

Blair stopped the car at the entrance of the drive and looked around. Sighing at the beauty surrounding her, she willed herself to continue on, but suddenly Sean's face floated before her eyes, and she thought about Alice's cocktail party.

She wondered what Sean Mathias was really like. Was he the way she remembered him from the party? After seeing him that one time, so perfectly tailored in his blue suit, talking so animatedly with the blonde, she was certain he was everything she'd read about him in the newspapers and magazines—a playboy author with a thousand conquests behind him and a thousand more ahead.

But as she thought these things, Blair had to concede that Sean's rugged good looks had even attracted her—for a brief moment. She believed, too, that he was like his writing: deep, strong and intensely passionate.

Blair shook the vision from her eyes. Not once since Brian's death had Blair found herself attracted to another man. And intuitively Blair knew she could not test her vulnerability with a lady-killer like Sean Mathias. But then another more logical thought cropped up. *Why would he want to make me his next conquest?* Blair was realistic enough to understand that she was not a glamorous and exotic type like the blonde whom Sean had been with at the party, nor did she want to be.

Knowing that she could not delay any longer, Blair glanced into the rearview mirror to check her makeup. Earlier, after registering at a small motel, Blair had changed into fresh clothing. She'd reapplied her lipstick and added a dab of rouge to her cheeks.

Finally, Blair put the car into gear and drove toward the brick and wood house. When she had stopped the car and shut the engine off, her pulse raced quickly. Taking a deep and calming breath, she opened the car door and stepped out. As she walked toward the front door, she looked at the scenery. The house was on a small ridge overlooking the Delaware River. Pausing, Blair gazed at the magnificence of the sight and thought that it should be painted by an artist who appreciated nature's vast beauty.

Before she reached the door, it swung open and the tall author stepped out. His angular face was capped by jet-black hair. His dark brown eyes searched Blair's face for a moment before a smile softened his features.

"Welcome, Miss Sanders. Did you have a good trip?" he asked in a husky voice.

"Mrs. Sanders," Blair replied as she closed the remaining distance and offered him her hand.

"Mrs. Sanders," he corrected himself as he took her hand in a gentle yet firm grip.

Blair was aware of the warmth of his hand. She quickly withdrew hers. "The trip was fine," she said in answer to his earlier question.

"Good. Please come inside," he offered, stepping out of her path to allow her to pass.

As she did, her hip unintentionally brushed against his upper thigh, and she felt something akin to an electric charge. Moving quickly inside, Blair covered her unease with a smile as she turned to watch him close the door.

"Oh," Sean said, turning to look at her before the door was completely closed, "I almost forgot your suitcase. Shall I get it?"

"I've already checked into a motel not far from here," Blair informed him in a stiffer tone than she'd meant to use.

Sean gazed at her for a moment before eloquently shrugging. "Why go to the expense of a motel? I told Alice there was more than enough room for you here," he said.

"Alice told me of your kind offer," she began, trying to explain the way she felt without giving him any offense, "but I prefer the motel.... I like my privacy," she added inanely.

"However you're most comfortable," Sean replied politely. "Would you like some coffee, or perhaps a glass of wine?"

"Coffee would be nice," Blair said as she followed him to a spacious country kitchen. Sean gestured toward a large oak table, surrounded by four oak-and-cane chairs.

"Have a seat, coffee will be ready in a moment." With that, he went to the sink and began to fill a kettle with water.

While he worked, Blair looked around. The kitchen was not just large, she realized, it was huge. The ceiling was supported by dark wooden beams, and four nice-size windows gave the room a bright, fresh look. The floor was tiled with large terra-cotta squares, and the cabinets and counters were all pale oak.

Then Blair fixed her focus on Sean, who was measuring out the coffee and putting it into a filter basket. He was dressed in a cordovan sweater that covered a blue shirt. Chocolate slacks hugged his slim hips, and brown loafers made the picture of a country gentleman complete.

Turning suddenly, Sean riveted Blair with an open gaze. "Do you believe in love?" he asked.

Blair drew in a deep breath at his unexpected question and the power emanating from his eyes. "I'm not sure I understand the question."

"It's not a complicated question, Mrs. Sanders," he said. "Do you believe in love?"

Blair's mouth turned strangely dry as she held Sean's stare. "Yes," she whispered.

"Good. If you didn't, you wouldn't be able to do this research."

Blair bristled at his words. Her neck arched stiffly, and her eyes narrowed. The warmth of a blush rose to her cheeks, but before she could force it away, Sean spoke again.

"I've offended you."

"Yes, you have," she said, biting off each word as if they, and not he, had been responsible for her anger. "I'm a professional. What I do, I do better than anyone else. And whether I believe in love or not will not impair my ability to do my job!"

Sean studied Blair's face for a moment longer. "That's not always true," he told her in a level voice. "Someone whose emotions were neatly tied up and hidden away could not do what is necessary for my research. An open mind and a willingness to seek out the unknown are what's necessary."

Blair's thoughts reeled under the impact of Sean's words and stare. The implication of what he had said, as well as what he had not said, made her suddenly afraid. *He couldn't mean that he expects me to act out a love affair of some sort,* she wondered. *Stop this foolishness,* she commanded herself. *Stop reading things into what he says.* Suddenly, Blair realized that it was a combination of her own defensiveness and Sean Mathias's overconfident manner that was making her hear the worst in what he said. And once again she felt her cheeks burning.

"If you doubt my abilities, why did you insist that I do your research personally?"

"I don't doubt your abilities, *Mrs.* Sanders. What I'm trying to learn is about your emotions."

"*Mr.* Mathias, my emotions are my concern, not yours. And the water is boiling," she informed him in a tight voice.

Taken off guard, Sean turned to see steam rising from the kettle's spout. "So it is," he murmured, "along with you."

Blair pretended not to hear his last words while she watched him pour the water through the filter. Her thoughts, like the steam that rose into the air, flew madly in all directions. *Why is he doing this? What kind of a game is he playing?*

Sean carried the two mugs to the table and placed one in front of Blair. "Milk or sugar?" he asked, but he realized that she had not heard him.

Blair followed the steam rising from the coffee mug until she met Sean's questioning eyes and became aware that he had spoken to her. "Excuse me?"

"Milk or sugar?"

"Neither."

"Ah, a woman after my own heart," he said lightly.

"Hardly," Blair retorted before she could control her tongue. She watched Sean raise one eyebrow, and then breathed a sigh of relief when he sat without speaking.

"You're very pretty," Sean said after taking a sip of coffee. Although he saw her grow angry again, he smiled gently, raising his palm to hold her comment back. "Don't get upset. I'm simply giving you a compliment and telling the truth at the same time."

But Blair's anger was unabated. "Is that another requirement to do your research? That I be pretty? Does the fact that I've kept my body in good physical shape also merit this work?" she asked angrily.

"No, that's a bonus. May I call you Blair?"

For some reason, Blair's anger disintegrated under Sean's suddenly boyish smile, and she found herself nodding. Then the sparkle in his eyes changed from merriment into something else, and Blair felt it in a stronger way than she should have.

"And will you call me Sean? I prefer to work on a first-name basis. After all, Mrs. Sanders and Mr. Mathias does seem a bit stuffy."

"Then I take it you still want me to do the research?" Blair asked, still not certain of exactly what was happening.

"That was never in doubt," Sean replied, smiling again.

Blair watched laugh lines spring outward from his eyes as a random ray of sunlight came through one of the large windows to wash across his face. In that instant, Blair saw just how good-looking he was.

"Mr., uh, Sean, could we talk about the work you want me to do? After all, that is why I'm here," Blair said in an effort to halt the softening of her mood toward him. *What's happening to me,* she asked herself.

"Why do you still wear your wedding band?" Sean asked, his eyes going to her left hand.

Blair lifted her hand from the table to stare at the gold band that was as much a part of her as her skin. "Because I choose to," she told him, her voice sounding loud and defensive in the confines of the kitchen. Alice must have told him. Sean's next words confirmed that very fact to her.

"I see," Sean said as he studied her face again. "That is as much the reason for asking you to do the research as your ability is, and I'm well aware of the work you do. Blair, I know about your background. I made it a point to learn about you after our brief conversation at the cocktail party."

Willing herself to keep control of her emotions, she stared openly at him, doing her best to hide her discomfort at his latest revelation. She was surprised that Sean had remembered her at all from the few moments they'd talked at Alice's party.

Blair tried to organize her suddenly confused thoughts, and only succeeded in getting angry.

"What right do you have to look into my past?" she demanded in a tight voice. Pushing herself away from the table, Blair stood, unwilling to let herself remain in a situation over which she had no control.

Seeing the anger on her face, Sean stood too. "Blair," he said in a gentle voice, "I talked to Alice about you because I had to know if you were truly capable of doing this research. Please sit down and hear me out."

It wasn't his words that brought her back to the chair; rather, it was the look in his deep brown eyes that compelled her to stay. She spoke a few seconds after she sat down. "The research?"

"The research is about love," Sean told her.

"I thought it was about reincarnation."

"That too," he said. As he spoke, Blair was soon lost in the smooth resonance of his voice. Listening to the words roll from his tongue, Blair was totally intrigued.

Sean was writing a book based on five case histories of lovers who had been reincarnated. He told Blair of the present-day people and of their experiences under hypnosis. What her job would be, he informed her, was to research the actuality of their past lives—find evidence that these people really did exist in other lifetimes. She learned, too, that Sean had specifically chosen people whose past lives could be documented within the North American continent rather than in Europe.

"But for today I think dinner would be in order."

Belatedly, Blair realized that she had been so absorbed in Sean's story that she hadn't noticed that the sun had set, and dusk was darkening the kitchen windows. Then, as if she were returning to life, Blair heard the sounds of hundreds of crickets welcoming the onset of night.

"Would you like to go back to your motel and change or go the way you are, which I might add, is lovely?"

Blair held back another retort to his words. "If you're not changing, I see no reason for me to."

Sean took Blair to a small country inn overlooking the Delaware, not five miles from his house. They ate an excellent dinner and the conversation was both lively and unantagonistic. By the time dinner was over, Blair was able to drop some of her air of reserve and began to feel more relaxed than she had in a long time. She enjoyed listening to his stories and was starting to get a sense of the man behind the writer.

Over coffee, Blair agreed to Sean's suggestion that he pick her up in the morning, rather than returning with her to his house that night for her car. She'd be spared having to drive back to the motel alone and on an unfamiliar road.

When they left the restaurant, Blair leaned her head against the leather headrest and, through barely opened eyes, gazed surreptitiously at Sean.

The entire evening had conspired to make her drop her guard: she could not help but notice the change in the atmosphere between them since her arrival at his house earlier that day.

The low glow of the dashboard lights illuminated Sean's features and once again Blair became extremely aware of how handsome the author was. *Too good-looking for my own good,* she thought.

But when she closed her eyes to cut off this ghostly vision, a new feeling began to grow within her. Before she could think about it, the car slowed and a moment later stopped.

Sean shut off the ignition and glanced at Blair. Her face was relaxed, her eyes closed. She looked peaceful and beautiful, and he did not want to change this moment. But he knew he must. Opening his door, Sean spoke. "We're here."

Blair stared into the darkness. "I know."

Sean walked around the car and opened her door, offering his hand to help her out of the low-slung car. When she took his hand, a flash of heat raced across her palm, but she did her best to ignore it.

Sean escorted her to her room and stood behind her while she unlocked the door. When she withdrew the key from the lock and turned to say good-night, her breath caught. His dark eyes were gazing down at her; his handsome features were almost overwhelming.

Even before she felt his hands settle gently on her shoulders, she knew he was going to kiss her.

Her stomach tightened painfully, and her heart raced. She forced herself to moisten her too-dry lips and then stepped back. Blair shook her head. "No," she whispered.

"No?" he echoed, his hands holding her shoulders firmly.

"Don't kiss me, Sean."

Despite her words, Sean leaned toward her.

"No!" she commanded, forcing the strange reactions of her body away. "If you want me to work for you, never, never try that again!"

Sean shook his head slowly and lifted his hands from her shoulders. "I can't promise that. And, Blair, I don't think you want me to either."

Before she could speak, he said, "I'll pick you up at eleven." Without another word, Sean went to his car.

Blair stared at his retreating back.

As she heard the sound of the car's engine, she finally shook herself free of the paralysis that had been gripping her and went into her room, locking the door behind her.

While Sean negotiated the familiar road, his mind was anywhere but on his driving. Ever since he'd met Blair Sanders, he had been unable to get her out of his mind. The two minutes he'd spent talking to her at Alice's party had told him that she was someone special—someone he wanted to know better.

Her green-flecked eyes had been mysteriously veiled, yet at the same time he'd seen flashes of fire building within them. Her short, curly hair had accented the perfection of delicate features, and a slender neck. When he'd spoken to her, he'd seen a vein beneath the porcelain skin of her neck pulsing with the even beat of her heart.

Everything about Blair—her proud carriage and smoothly curved body, the mystery within her eyes, the understated but vibrant beauty that surrounded her like an aura—had called out to Sean in a way no woman had ever called to him before.

When he had asked Alice to arrange for Blair to do the research on the reincarnation book, Alice had told him that Blair would not work with him. Alice was sure that Blair would do the research, but she would not work personally with him.

"Besides," Alice had added, "she's not your type."

"Not my type?" he'd asked sarcastically. "Alice, you're reading your own publicity releases. Blair Sanders is, if you must use that particular word, my type. You know me well enough to know that I don't play games."

"Why Blair?" Alice asked.

"I don't know, Alice. All I do know is that I want her to be a part of my life."

"You just met her tonight.... No, you didn't really meet her."

"Alice, help me."

"She's fragile, Sean. She's not a part of your world. I don't want to see her hurt, she's been through enough already."

"I won't hurt her."

"You really do like her, don't you?" Alice had asked.

Sean had merely nodded his head.

"All right, I'll work it out somehow. Just don't rush her. Don't chase her away, please."

Sean shrugged away the memory of the night of the party as he crossed the wooden bridge. Alice had cautioned him not to rush her, and all he'd done, since the moment she had arrived, had been exactly that.

Yet Sean sensed that his feelings were not one-sided. He believed that she was responding to him. Then another thought rose to taunt him just as he pulled the car to a stop before his house.

Sean remembered the look in Blair's eyes when he had been about to kiss her. Fear, he realized belatedly. *She's afraid of me.* "Time," he whispered, "give her time."

Golden sunshine, accompanied by the sounds of birds, woke Blair from a deep sleep. Slowly, luxuriating within the tranquil feeling of waking, Blair stretched and yawned. Then she looked at the small travel alarm clock on the nightstand. It was ten-thirty.

What had happened to the alarm, she wondered, as she forced herself to move swiftly. Picking up the clock, she saw she'd failed to set it the previous night. Shaking her head at her forgetfulness, Blair left the comfort of the bed and went into the bathroom and turned on the shower. She only had a half hour before Sean would arrive.

With the small room filling with steam, Blair stepped under the water. *Had last night really happened,* she asked herself, thinking of that frozen moment in time when Sean had almost kissed her. *His nerve infuriates me! His ego and his overconfidence are too much. I should leave now.*

But Blair knew she couldn't leave. Yesterday had decided that. Everything Sean had told her about the book had completely entrapped her. She also realized that Alice had been right. This research job was a challenge. Blair wanted to learn about the people of whom Sean was writing, and she wanted to know more of their past lives and loves.

Blair poured shampoo into her palm and then massaged it into her hair while she thought about the research. After rinsing the lather from her hair, she stepped out of the shower and dried herself with a terry towel.

At five minutes before eleven, Blair finished dressing. Standing in front of the mirror, she critically eyed the spring outfit she'd picked. The cotton lavender sweater fit nicely, sloping gently over her breasts without overemphasizing their fullness. The denim skirt she'd chosen hugged her narrow waist and accented her trim stomach before ending at her knees. Leather thong sandals encased her feet, adding a scant inch to her five feet four inches.

Satisfied that she looked appropriate for her meeting with Sean, Blair used her fingers to arrange her still damp curls. Just as she finished, there was a knock on the door. "Coming," she called.

When she opened the door, her breath caught. Sean was outlined by the sun, a bold smile on his face. He was dressed casually, wearing a pale blue knit shirt and dark blue slacks. The shirt accented all too well his smoothly proportioned chest. *Stop,* Blair commanded herself silently.

"Good morning," Sean said, his voice just a bit huskier than he'd wanted it to sound. His eyes swept across her face, drinking in its softly radiant beauty. "You look lovely in the morning."

Blair shook her head. "I thought we settled all of that last night. We're supposed to work today."

"Exactly," Sean replied, offering her his arm. "Shall we?"

"As soon as I get my things," she told him. She retrieved her purse and attaché case from the small table and, after locking the door, let him escort her to his car.

"It's such a beautiful day I thought I'd leave the top down. Do you mind?" he asked as they walked to the sleek sports car and he opened the door for her. Without waiting for a reply, he went to the driver's side and got in.

Moments later they were on the road, and Blair was soon enjoying the sun above and the wind blowing through her hair. She only wished that she didn't have to work. She would enjoy spending the day just relaxing.

But when she realized that Sean was driving past his house, a thread of anxiety rose within her mind. "Where are we going?"

Sean answered her question with one of his own. "Did you have breakfast yet?"

Blair shook her head.

"I didn't think so. First breakfast, then work."

Blair shrugged. *I should relax,* she told herself, remembering that Sean was paying for her time, breakfast and all.

Ten minutes later, Sean slowed the car and then pulled off the road. He drove carefully across a wide expanse of grass, stopping at the onset of a small grove of tall pine trees not twenty feet from the bank of the Delaware River.

"Breakfast," he announced.

"I don't usually eat fish in the morning."

Sean smiled secretively and got out of the car. "If madame will assist," he said, cocking his head to the side before he went to the rear of the car.

Blair left the car and went to the back. Once there, Sean handed her a wicker picnic basket and took out a neatly folded blanket. Still without speaking, they walked to the edge of the river.

"This is one of the most beautiful places in the Northeast, especially for breakfast," Sean informed her as he spread the blanket on the ground. Taking the basket from her, he motioned her to sit.

Moving gracefully, Sean opened the basket and put out two plates and a thermos. Next came the cups, followed by a napkin-covered woven basket that smelled of freshly baked bread. Suddenly, Blair saw just how practiced and smooth all of Sean's movements were. Just as suddenly, her anxiety increased.

Before another moment had passed, Sean had poured the coffee and seated himself across from Blair. "Is everything satisfactory, madame?" he asked in a patently false French accent.

"Everything is perfect," Blair said with a smile. "It must be all the experience you've had," she added.

"And where would we be without experience to teach us?" Sean asked, doing his best to ignore the warning ring within him that her words had triggered.

Blair shook her head. "I'm afraid you're wasting your expertise on me. Besides not being your *type*, I'm not the least interested in a fling with a famous writer,'' Blair stated, deciding that it would be best to place all her cards on the table. But she had not expected the reaction that her words caused.

Sean's smiling, pleasant countenance changed to one of strained intensity. His deep eyes were flashing dangerously by the time she'd finished speaking, and his hands had become knotted fists. Above her were the sounds of birds in the trees; behind her the river moved swiftly; but none of that mattered, for all she was aware of was the fury on his face.

Chapter Three

Wake up, Mrs. Sanders! You may want to live in a dream world, but you're in the real one. Do you think that every man you meet wants to have a fling with you? And who the hell are you to tell me what my *type* is?"

Blair flushed hotly. The blood rushing through her cheeks seared her with the knowledge of her mistake. She wanted to run away and hide, but she knew she could not do that. "I—I'm sorry if I've offended you," she said hesitantly, "but your reputation preceded you."

"My reputation?" he asked, the surprise registering on his face replaced the anger of seconds before. "What does my reputation have to do with this breakfast?"

Blair was confused by his obvious surprise, yet wary at the same time. "Really, Sean, you're a well-known ladies' man. Your affairs are written up in all the newspapers. Why else would I have said what I did?" As Blair stared at him, still trying to recover from what had already happened, something followed that took her even more by surprise.

For a brief instant the knife edge of rage sliced through Sean's mind, propelled by her words. But he pushed that emotion aside as his intuition led him along the right path. "Are you that afraid of me?" he whispered. Before she could respond, Sean moved toward her. "Don't be."

Under the confusion of her thoughts, Blair remained rooted to the spot. When Sean sank down next to her and reached out to cup her face between his palms, she stiffened and tried to pull away, but could not.

His face was only inches from hers, and she could feel the sweet warmth of his breath washing across her skin. "Please, Sean..."

"Don't be afraid of me, Blair. And don't fight your own emotions. I can feel you tremble at my touch. I felt it last night, and I feel it now."

To her horror, Blair could not fight him. One hand was pressed against his chest as if she were pushing him away. Her other hand hung limply at her side and she could not summon the strength to lift it, even when his face drew closer to hers.

Suddenly, his lips touched hers. A jolt raced across her mouth; her breath was trapped in her chest. But Sean's lips never pressed harshly upon hers; they merely lingered for a brief and gentle second before drawing away.

Blair watched him, almost falling into the endless depths of his soft brown eyes. Her heart was racing and her breathing had deepened. A slow, insistant heat was rising within her, and the heat, as much as anything else that had happened so far, shook her with its message of response.

I can't let this happen, she told herself. *I can't!* As she gazed at him, she tried to call up Brian's image. She willed herself to see her husband alive and standing near her, but she failed. All she could do was feel Sean's fleeting kiss upon her lips.

After an eternal moment, Sean released Blair's face and exhaled softly. "Don't tell me you're not my type, not until you know what that is."

Blair closed her eyes and tried her hardest to blot out the intensity of his words and gaze, all the while knowing that she had responded to him on every level and that she had suddenly found herself wanting him. "Please," she whispered, her voice reflecting how deeply shaken she was, "please don't do that again."

When Sean did not reply, Blair opened her eyes. He was still staring at her, his brown eyes holding her in thrall. But even as she felt this strong power of his, she saw a change come over him. His eyes lost their intensity, and a gentler glow filled them.

"Shall we eat?"

Blair nodded and without speaking, lifted her coffee cup with both hands because she was afraid that if she used only one hand, he would see how badly that hand was trembling. And she did not want him to see how he was affecting her.

Standing, Sean smiled at her for the first time since their words had grown so heated, and then went back to where he'd been sitting. When he lifted his coffee cup and sipped at it, he began to relax.

"The reason I brought you here was so that after we ate we could begin work. I can't think of a more pleasant spot for work."

Mutely, Blair nodded in agreement.

As Blair dressed, she had to admit to herself that the day had gone quite well—at least after the tense start at breakfast. They had worked all day, sitting in the pine grove next to the river, and by six Sean had driven her back to the motel. When he'd dropped her off, he'd told her he would be back at eight and that they would be having dinner with friends of his if she didn't mind.

She hadn't minded, and had told him so. And as she adjusted the strap of her dress, she realized he would be there soon. She was also glad that she'd brought some outfits that would be appropriate for the evenings, especially this new dress.

The conservatively cut dress, a deep cinnamon shade, was of a lightweight material. The dress fell smoothly, curving where she did but not hugging her body suggestively. Turning sideways, Blair glanced at her image in approval. Then she moved closer to the mirror and inspected her face. Because of the hours spent under the sun today, Blair had used no base. She liked the healthy, rosy tint that suffused her cheeks, and had used only a small amount of green shadow on her eyelids to emphasize the green flecks in her eyes. A hint of mascara finished off the look.

What am I doing?

Slowly, Blair walked away from the mirror and sat on the edge of the bed. Her hands were in her lap, her right hand holding her left. She looked down at her wedding band.

"Why, Brian?" she whispered. "Why did you leave me?" Tears threatened to rise. Defiantly, Blair shook her head, refusing to allow sadness to plague her again. The battle lasted only a few short seconds, and when it was over, Blair was dry-eyed.

Blair went to the closet, took out a white cotton wrap and draped it across her shoulders before going to the door. She needed to be outside, not closed in by walls, when Sean arrived.

Outside, Blair's mood eased while she breathed in the clean air. A moment later she heard the distinctively low rumble of a sports car and turned just as Sean pulled into the parking lot and coasted to a stop near her.

He shut off the engine and got out. His eyes met Blair's and then wandered candidly over her length. He smiled when he drew close to her. "Thank you."

"For what?" she asked, puzzled by his comment.

"For looking so lovely. You do."

"I... Thanks," she finally replied. Gazing at him, she almost nodded approvingly at his beige slacks, a light blue shirt open at the collar and a royal-blue sports jacket. "You look lovely too." The moment she said it, she flushed. "Do you always wear blue?" she asked to cover up her embarrassment.

"I like the color," he said simply as he led her to the car and opened the door for her.

Pausing before she got in, she looked at Sean, who was on his way to the driver's side. "It suits you." Drawing the wrap tighter about her shoulders, she sat down.

"Shall I close the top?"

"No, I like the night air. About dinner," she asked as he started the car, "who are your friends?"

"Ah, the first signs of relenting... She wants to know about my friends. Love..."

Blair held back her angry retort long enough to realize that he was teasing her. She smiled suddenly and waited.

Sean didn't react to her unexpected restraint or to the radiant smile she was so suddenly favoring him with, even though he wanted to. "Paul and Erica Lowery are the people we're visiting tonight. Paul and I grew up together. I became a writer, Paul became Erica's husband."

Blair thought she detected a hidden note beneath Sean's words and wondered what had caused it. "That's his occupation?"

Sean laughed. "Vocation actually, but he does work hard at it when he's not teaching school."

The soft glow from the dashboard illuminated Sean's features and Blair experienced a strange sensation forming in her stomach; she closed her eyes for a moment in an effort to will it away.

Sean, glancing quickly at Blair, saw her eyes were shut. "Are you all right?"

"Fine. I was just thinking." Suddenly she realized what the strange feeling was and understood as well as the undertone of his earlier words. "Are you in love with her?"

"Her?" Sean asked, trying to figure out what or who Blair was talking about.

"Erica," she blurted.

"What?" Sean said, half turning to look at her.

The car weaved briefly, and Blair was aware of how startled Sean had been. Only when the car was running smoothly again did Sean speak.

"Why did you ask that?"

Blair shrugged her shoulders but did not look at him. "Intuition perhaps. But more because of the way you said her name," Blair admitted truthfully. From the corner of her eye, Blair saw Sean smiling broadly.

"Yes, I do love Erica," he told her.

For no reason at all, Blair's stomach knotted. She forced herself to stare at the road and to not allow any thought at all to come into her mind.

"But," Sean added after a moment's silence, "I'm not in love with Erica. Although I will admit I'm a little jealous of Paul because he's so happy. No, I love Erica as a sister."

Blair's tight stomach eased; she breathed a low sigh. "That's very nice," she said. "I wouldn't think of you as someone with such tender emotions."

Sean tensed and his hands tightened on the steering wheel. When he spoke, his voice was raspy. "Because of my *reputation*?"

Only after hearing his words did Blair realize that she had voiced what she'd meant to be only a thought, and she could not meet his eyes. "I'm sorry, Sean," she whispered.

Sean refused to accept her apology. "Put your defenses down, lady! Let yourself enjoy this evening. I won't attack you! I wouldn't want to impose my *reputation* on my friends."

Blair steeled herself against the force of his sarcasm and tried not to let it burrow into her. "I really am sorry."

After another five minutes of silence, Sean pulled the car to a stop in front of a stone-faced two-story colonial house. In the driveway were two cars; near the garage were two bicycles lying on their sides.

Before Sean and Blair reached the steps leading to the house, the front door opened and two children ran out. Sean stopped and bent. A second later his arms were filled with the giggling little girls. Blair watched as he kissed both girls and held them close.

Their laughter rang pleasantly, causing yet another strange stirring within Blair's stomach. Sean looked so right with the little girls that it shocked her to think of him as a father.

"Blair Sanders, I'd like you to meet Jennifer and Lauren Lowery." When the girls turned their big blue eyes on Blair, she realized that they were identical twins.

"Good evening Jennifer, Lauren."

"Are you Sean's girlfriend?" asked the twin on the left.

"Are you going to marry him?" asked the one on the right.

"Are you two going to behave yourselves tonight?" came an authoritative and yet gentle voice. Blair looked up at her rescuer and knew it was the twins' mother. Erica Lowery was as beautiful as her daughters, with the same large blue eyes and silky blond hair.

Stepping forward, Erica offered her hand. "I'm Erica, as I'm sure you've guessed. I'm pleased to meet you, Blair. I've heard so much about you."

Confused by Erica's statement, Blair willed the smile to stay on her face. "Nothing flattering, I'm sure," she replied. Erica raised her eyebrows questioningly as she looked from Blair to Sean and back again.

"Okay, girls, you can let go of Uncle Sean now."

"Awww..." the twins cried in unison.

"Come on, ladies," Sean said as he scooped them off the ground and carried them toward the front door. At the same time, Erica's arm went through Blair's, and she escorted her into the house.

"They're both in love with him," Erica said of the twins. "They have been since they could say his name."

"They're adorable. How old are they?"

"Six. And adorable is a temporary situation at best," Erica said good-naturedly. "I understand you're working with Sean on his new book," she said when they entered the house.

Blair nodded as she looked around. "You have a lovely home," Blair said, changing the subject as they entered the large living room. She always made it a point never to discuss her work, as it was a private matter between her and her client. The living room, decorated in soft earth tones, was accented by brightly colored paintings. The furniture looked as comfortable as it was tasteful.

"Hello, I'm Paul," announced a deep voice that drew her eyes toward the archway and the man striding toward her. When he reached the newcomers, he took Blair's hand in his and shook it firmly. Paul was only an inch taller than Erica, and Blair sensed that they were, indeed, a perfect couple. They looked right together, they fit.

"Can I get you a drink? Some wine?" Paul asked.

"Thank you."

"Erica?" he asked. Erica nodded and Paul started out. Suddenly the squeals of the twins reached them and Paul glanced quickly at Erica.

"Girls!" Erica called, "time for bed." She smiled at Blair and guided her to the sofa even as the twins cried in anguish.

Then they heard the sounds of little feet on the carpet. When the twins reached them, the girls kissed Erica, smiled shyly at Blair and went over to where Paul was pouring the wine. They waited patiently until he finished and bent down to them.

"Good night princess," Paul said as he kissed Jennifer, and then repeated both the words and the deed with Lauren.

"Good night," the girls chorused as they started toward the stairs.

"Get yourselves ready and I'll be up to tuck you in," Erica promised. But even as she spoke, the girls turned toward Sean, who was just entering the room, and looked up at him with their large, pleading eyes.

Then the girls looked at their mother for a moment and back at Sean. Blair couldn't resist a quiet laugh at the sight. As if echoing her own thoughts, she heard Erica's sigh.

"All right, get upstairs and Uncle Sean will tuck you in."

"And tell us a story," they chorused.

"And tell you a story," Sean agreed.

Paul served the drinks, handing the first to Blair and the second to Erica. Sean took the third glass and raised it toward his friends in a silent toast. After taking a sip of the cool wine, he placed the glass on a coaster.

"I'll be back in a few minutes," he said.

"Make it a short story," Paul pleaded. "It's hard to match your long ones...especially after a bad day at school."

"A short one," Sean agreed. A moment later he was gone.

Paul took another sip of wine and then favored Blair with a smile. "How long will you be staying?"

"I'm not certain," Blair responded. "Another day or two at the most. Then I have to get back to the city and start on the research Sean will need." On cue with her last word, a timer bell sounded.

Paul stood quickly. "Excuse me, but duty calls.... Onion soup is my specialty," he added as he left the living room, wineglass in hand.

"Paul only cooks his specialties, I'm left with the rest," Erica said with a smile that contradicted the harshness of her words. After taking another sip of wine, Erica gazed directly at Blair. "I must tell you that I was surprised when Sean said he was bringing a guest. You must be very special to him."

Blair was momentarily flustered by Erica's comment. "I'm only working for him," she protested, wondering what Erica Lowery must be thinking.

"Really? After the way I saw him look at you, I'm surprised. You see, Sean has never brought a woman into this house. And as the girls' godfather, he's here often."

Only one of Erica's statements fully filtered into her mind. "Looks at me?" Blair whispered as a flush crept into her cheeks.

"If I've offended you..." Erica began, but Blair waved away her apology.

"No. It's just that I'm here to work with Sean, that's all."

"I see," Erica said, but Blair didn't think she understood at all. Erica's next words confirmed that thought. "Don't let his public image put you off. He's not what he appears to be."

Instead of speaking and getting herself even more deeply involved in this apparent misunderstanding, Blair picked up her wineglass from the coffee table and took a sip. As she did, she saw Erica's eyes widen, and then the blond woman shook her head slowly.

"I think I just embarrassed myself," Erica admitted. "I didn't realize you were married," she said as she looked at Blair's wedding band. "Please forgive me."

"I'm widowed," Blair explained in a low voice, her eyes fixed firmly on the wineglass.

"How long has it been?"

"Four years." As she said the words, she could feel Erica's penetrating gaze and she lifted her eyes to meet the other woman's.

"You loved him deeply. I can see it in your eyes."

Blair could only nod.

"It must have been hard on you. I can't imagine life without Paul." Erica stood suddenly and went to the bar. Picking up the bottle of wine, she returned to the couch and filled Blair's glass again. "I really am a busybody, and I'm sorry if I've made you feel uncomfortable."

"It's all right," Blair said, deeply affected by Erica's sensitivity. "Really it is."

Just as Erica sat down again, Paul returned to the living room. "As soon as Sean tears himself away from the girls, we'll eat."

"Did someone say eat?" Sean asked as he too entered the room.

"Shall we?" Erica offered, as she stood to lead everyone into the dining room.

After a delicious dinner everyone was relaxing on the sofa, watching the orange flames lick upward in the stone fireplace. The small crowd had taken their coffee to the living room, and Paul, at Erica's insistence, had started a fire. A few minutes later Paul had ducked into the kitchen. When he'd returned, it was with an old-fashioned corn popper. Then Paul made several quarts of popcorn, which the four of them devoured as if they hadn't eaten a large meal a short time before.

Blair, sitting only inches from Sean, was half relaxed and half wary. He had been warm and attentive without playing the tense games she was used to from him, and Blair appreciated this respite. Yet his very nearness was the thing that disturbed her. She could feel a low heat emanating from his body even as she felt another form of heat coming from the fireplace. That awareness gave her cause to again wonder why she was reacting so strongly to him.

The chiming of a grandfather clock startled Blair from her thoughts. Looking at her watch, she saw it was midnight. Then she felt Sean's eyes on her.

"We have an appointment early in the morning," she reminded him.

Sean nodded and reluctantly drew his eyes from her. For the past few minutes he had been studying her, content with the lull in the conversation and thankful that Blair seemed to be more at ease in his company.

But he knew the evening was over and stood slowly, stretching as he did. When Blair stood, so did Paul and Erica, and together the four walked toward the front door. There, Erica retrieved Blair's wrap and handed it to her.

When they stepped outside, Blair breathed deeply of the cool night air and drew the wrap tighter about her shoulders. In the driveway, while Sean secured the sports car's top, Blair said goodbye to Erica and Paul.

Paul shook Blair's hand and smiled. Then he went over to give Sean a hand.

"It's really been a pleasure meeting you," Erica said when they were alone. "And if you're ever in this part of the state again, please stop by."

"Thank you for the dinner and the company," Blair replied, knowing the impossibility of ever taking her up on her offer.

"You're welcome," she said. Then Erica's voice turned into a whisper that only she and Blair could hear. "Don't try to fool yourself for too long."

Stiffening, Blair tried to dismiss Erica's words, but Erica would not let her.

"Don't be offended. I'm outspoken to a fault, and I liked you the moment I met you. I know it's none of my business, but Blair, Sean doesn't date often, and I've never seen Sean look at another woman the way he looks at you. And you..." But Erica stopped herself from going any further.

"I... Good night," Blair managed to say. A moment later she turned and walked to the car, her thoughts swirling like a confused whirlpool.

Once she was seated in the car, she watched Sean embrace Paul and then Erica before he joined her and drove away.

"I hope you enjoyed the evening," Sean said.

"It was lovely, and so are Paul and Erica."

A comfortable silence descended upon them as the road flew by and the hum of the tires lulled Blair's eyes closed. A few moments later she felt Sean shift in his seat. When she opened her eyes slightly, she saw him take one hand from the steering wheel, and immediately sensed its destination.

When his hand covered hers, warmth spread quickly along her arm and stopped the protest that had barely begun to form. She closed her eyes again and leaned her head back.

Blair tried to think of anything but the hand that was on hers. She tried valiantly but failed as the warmth continued to spread and was soon threatening to engulf her entire body.

Suddenly, Erica's words rose within her mind. "I have never seen Sean look at another woman the way he looks at you." *She's wrong. She has to be!* Blair was certain that Sean looked at all women the same way. Willing her thoughts to ease, Blair tried to concentrate on the sounds of the car.

Sean glanced briefly at Blair and smiled. She looked beautiful with her head tilted back and her eyes closed. Once again, the feelings that had stolen over him when he'd first seen her returned, and he sensed that there was a great deal at stake—his future. In that moment, Sean knew he must speak to her before it was too late. Exhaling deeply when he saw the lights of the motel, he returned his right hand to the steering wheel and slowed the car.

Blair's concentration was broken when Sean lifted his hand from hers and the car slowed. Reluctantly she opened her eyes and saw the bright neon sign of the motel looming close. After Sean pulled into a parking space, Blair straightened and started to reach for the door handle, but Sean's hand returned to cover hers.

"Blair. Wait," he asked.

Blair saw the serious set of his face. The way her name rolled from his lips sounded more like a caress than a word. "I've had a pleasant evening, thank you, Sean, but I'm tired and I'd like to go in."

Sean shook his head. "When I first saw you at the party, I had to meet you. I knew that you and Alice were friends—"

"We've already discussed this," she reminded him. Sean's hand tightened on hers; heat raced up her arm.

"Let me say what I have to," he asked, his eyes piercing her. Then he waited until he saw Blair's imperceptible nod. "She told me about you and even reminded me that you'd done work for me before, although I'd never met you. She didn't want to talk about you, but I made her. When I explained I wanted to see you socially, she said it would be impossible. I refused to accept that."

"It was the truth," Blair stated, unable to take her eyes from his face.

"I know. When she said you never dated, I cajoled her into offering you this job. I made her understand how important it was to me, and, Blair, it is very, very important."

Blair's heart was pounding hard, and her body was turning into liquid beneath Sean's penetrating gaze. The honesty of his words affected her deeply, and left no doubt as to his emotions. But she could not—would not—let herself respond to him.

Blinking, Blair tried her best to hold his gaze with her own. "Sean...I'm not ready for any involvements."

"Four years is too long to mourn, Blair. It's time to feel things again."

Within her mind, a trembling response to his words was awakened. Yet her anger, too, was sparked by his assumption that he knew what was best for her. Pulling her hand from beneath his, she shook her head adamantly.

"No, Sean, you don't have the right to speak to me this way." Blair took a deep, shuddering breath and said, "This was a mistake. I knew better than to accept this job. I'm sorry, Sean, but I can't continue. There...there will be no bill for my time," she added, feeling a little foolish for saying it.

Sean stared at her for several seconds. Then his lips grew into a taut line. "What are you talking about? Didn't you hear what I said?" he asked. He reached for and grasped her hand again, this time holding it tightly. "I don't want you out of my life. I hired you because I need the research done, but I also hired you to bring you closer to me, so that I could tell you how I felt."

"I heard what you said," Blair replied in a controlled voice. "But you apparently didn't hear what Alice told you. It was the truth Sean, I do not date. I want nothing more than to work and to be left alone!"

Sean shook his head fiercely, working hard to hold back the anger her denial brought out. "You can tell that to your friends, but you can't deceive me. Blair, don't lie to me...or to yourself."

Blair tried to free her hand from his, but found it was imprisoned tightly. Then his other hand went to her shoulder and drew her toward him. Time ground to a halt as their faces came closer together. She tried to protest, but before she could, time started again and his mouth was upon hers.

Suddenly her body betrayed her. The softness of his lips branded hers and made her almost cry out. Fire exploded deep within her when the heat of his lips became too intense to ignore. Lances of desire shot through her, and her lips parted under the insistence of the heated tip of his tongue. Blair felt herself lose control, her mind became fogged. But she forcefully reached within her for an anchor to stop her sinking mind, and as she found it and held on to it, she pulled away from him.

"No!" she shouted, tearing her mouth from his. Her body was trembling from the fearful reaction to the explosive kiss.

Moving quickly, Blair opened her door and jumped from the car. Behind her, she heard Sean get out and, a moment later, sensed him near while she searched frantically for the room key. Finding the key, she drew it from her purse just as Sean's hand reached her shoulder.

Whirling, Blair faced him again. "Leave me alone!" she pleaded.

"I can't," Sean said in a level voice, his eyes sweeping back and forth across her face. Then he cupped her chin with his hand. "Blair, I want you to stay. I need you to stay."

"No," Blair whispered, feeling the overpowering intensity pouring from his eyes. "I'm not ready yet," she pleaded as she pulled free of his hands.

"I'll wait, Blair," Sean stated, "but only for a little while. Think about me. Think about what we could have together," Sean said as he took the key from her trembling fingers and opened the door for her.

"I have to leave tomorrow," she told him.

Sean shook his head. "Stay, Blair. Stay for me and for yourself." Then Sean smiled. It was a gentle smile, not one of victory or superiority. "I'll pick you up at eight. Breakfast will be in a restaurant, I promise. Goodnight," he said quickly, before she could protest.

"Goodnight," she whispered to his retreating back, aware that she had not yet agreed to stay and uncertain whether she would.

Then she went inside the room and closed the door behind her. Ten minutes later she was in bed and ready to sleep.

But an hour later Blair was still wide awake, her mind racing through an insolvable maze. The memory of the passionate kiss was torturing her mind as heavily as it was her body. *Why am I reacting like this?* Not even Brian had set her body aflame the way just a single kiss from Sean had. *How can I let myself feel like this about him?*

And then one burning thought burst free within her mind. *Knowing how Sean affects me, how can I work with him and still remain faithful to Brian's memory?*

Blair came to the only decision she could. Tomorrow morning when Sean came for her, she would tell him in no uncertain terms that she could not work for or with him.

But the book, she asked herself, her thoughts again vacillating madly. The research work was incredible. Never before had she had the opportunity to gain this sort of knowledge. And she admitted that she was utterly fascinated by everything that Sean had told her and had already shown her. *Reincarnation... Was it really possible?*

Blair realized she was caught in a trap. She knew she should run away, run far and run fast, but she also wanted to learn more.

The strange conversation between her and Erica returned to her mind. *Could Sean be the man Erica thinks him? Or is he what I believe him to be?* With those last questions, Blair's eyes grew heavy and she gladly consigned herself to the escape of sleep.

Chapter Four

The day was slightly overcast, but it was warm. It had been a strange day, Blair thought, ethereal at best: a day filled with myriad activities that followed one after the other. But even the fast pace of the day seemed to have become only a dim memory as she relaxed luxuriously within the afternoon's warmth.

She and Sean were walking within a copse of trees, and Blair could not remember the point at which she had let her guard down with Sean, but she felt none of the pressing tensions that had been so constant a part of their relationship up to now. When she heard the low rumble of thunder, she looked up, not in fear, but to see if a storm would spoil the day.

"It's still far away," Sean said in reassurance.

They continued on, hand in hand, until Sean stopped beneath a giant oak. He turned to her, his hands rising to caress the sides of her neck. She shivered under his light touch but did not want him to stop.

Looking into his eyes, she took a deep, ragged breath. "Sean," she whispered. Whatever she was about to say was stopped when his lips covered hers and fire rippled along their surface. A low moan escaped her throat.

"No," she protested when his mouth left hers. "Please, Sean, it's wrong."

"I can't stop myself. I want you, Blair. I need you." Then he pulled her tighter against him.

Heat pulsed within her breasts as they were crushed to his muscular chest. His hands wandered along the contours of her back and stole away all her resistance. Unable to fight him any longer, she felt herself sinking to the grassy floor of the woodland. Thunder accented the meeting of their mouths. Soon their tongues wove together in a dance of passion and need.

His hands were everywhere, lighting fires of passion and desire that began to consume her body. Yet no matter what she told herself, she was powerless to stop his explorations, and worse, her own hands were caressing his smoothly muscled back.

Her mind spun crazily, and time itself seemed to expand and contract until she realized that their clothing was gone. Heat raced across her skin, searing her and releasing uncontrollable waves of desire.

Then his hands were caressing her breasts, and his mouth soon followed. Pinpricks of desire vibrated through her breasts the moment he took her nipple into his mouth.

Blair's back arched, and a low moan floated upward to the branches that stirred in the breeze. She did not feel the prickly blades of grass beneath her; she only felt the soft and gentle ministrations of Sean's experienced hands.

Experienced, her mind screamed, as deep within her very center an eruption of need sent her blood singing madly.

"No!" she cried, denying everything that was happening.

Suddenly the world exploded in a blaze of fury. "No!" Blair screamed, sitting up straight and hugging herself tightly.

Gone were the swaying branches of the oak tree. Beneath her was a bed, not the grassy ground. Her ragged breathing was loud as she looked around and realized that she was in the motel room and not with Sean.

"A dream," she whispered as relief flooded her mind. But her relief was not enough to stop the trembling of her hands or ease the still heavy sounds of her labored breathing.

This can't go on, she declared silently. *I have to leave tomorrow.*

Blair was feeling much better, albeit a little nervous, as she finished fixing her hair. After the previous night's bad dream and her decision not to continue working with Sean, she had been able to fall into a dreamless sleep and had awakened unexpectedly refreshed.

As she patted one stray curl into place, she heard Sean's horn. Her nerves hummed in response to the sound, but she willed herself to be calm and to keep up the determination that had finally allowed her to sleep so peacefully. Picking up her attaché case, she left the room to join him outside.

When she saw him, she experienced a momentary twinge of unease along with a flashing memory of her dream, but pushed them aside.

"Good morning," Sean said pleasantly.

Blair couldn't help but return his warm smile with one of her own. "It is a lovely morning," she agreed as she looked at the incredibly clear and blue sky, noting thankfully that it was far from overcast, as the sky in her dream had been.

"Hungry?" Sean asked.

Blair thought about it for a moment. She'd believed that her nerves would make her appetite disappear, but they hadn't. "Yes."

After getting into the car and driving the half mile into town, Sean parked directly in front of a small restaurant. "This is where yesterday's breakfast came from," he told her as they left the car.

The inside of the restaurant was rustic and only half-filled with people. Wooden tables and chairs dotted the room, and the air smelled delicious. Scents of fresh-baked bread, and sizzling bacon permeated the air, and Blair's stomach rumbled in response.

After they had seated themselves, a waitress came over with two cups of coffee and took their order. When she was gone and Blair had taken her first sip of the coffee, she called up her determination to do what she felt was necessary.

"I can't work for you," she stated bluntly. Strangely, she saw her words had no visible effect on Sean. "Did you hear me?"

"No. I'm deaf sometimes. That's how I'm able to write when people talk to me."

"That's selective hearing, not deafness."

"What?" he asked, his face blank.

"Stop it!" Blair commanded, feeling the first stirring of anger.

"Stop what?" Sean asked.

"That!" Blair half shouted.

"I can't stop what I don't know I'm doing, can I?" he asked innocently. Before Blair's anger could lash out again, the waitress appeared with their food. When she was gone, Blair saw that Sean was not looking at her; rather, he was already eating.

Shaking her head in annoyance, Blair began to eat too. Although her nerves had once again become tense, she realized that she was still hungry. When their intolerably silent breakfast was over, Blair tried once more to make him understand what she was saying.

"Sean, please listen to me," she asked in a low voice. "It won't work. You need two people to have an...an affair. And I won't be used by anyone."

Sean, fully aware of what was happening, raised his eyes to meet hers. He was sure that what he read within the hazel depths contradicted everything she was saying. "Oh?" he asked casually. Slowly, he raised his cup and took another sip of coffee without once taking his eyes from hers. "You mean you want a commitment?"

"No!" she said in exasperation, "I mean I won't see you socially."

"Only business then?" he asked in the same level voice he'd been using all morning.

"I..." she began, but stopped. She had been prepared to walk away from him completely, but something within his eyes would not let her go. Instead of severing their relationship, she found herself agreeing to continue to do his research. "Only business," she whispered at last.

Sean nodded. A slight smile eased his features. "I'm patient...sometimes. If you don't want to admit the attraction that we feel for each other, then I'll just have to wait a little longer until you can see how foolish you're being."

Despite her attempts to stay cool and logical, Sean's words freed the anger she had already been hard pressed to hold back. "Foolish? I'm being foolish?" Blair replied, her voice rising higher and higher with each word. She was suddenly aware that everyone in the restaurant was staring at them.

Refusing to acknowledge the spectacle she was making of herself, she stared at Sean. "Damn you for an egotistical, unfeeling..." Without completing her statement, she rose quickly. "I'm going back home, now!" she stated. Turning, she walked quickly out of the restaurant.

Behind her, Sean stood also and threw several bills on the table. His eyes were narrowed into dangerous slits as he watched her walk away from him. A moment later he too was through the door and striding along the sidewalk after her.

Sean knew that once again he'd overstepped his own loosely placed boundaries, and the minute he'd spoken, he'd known it was a mistake. Yet his own anger welled up quickly at her much too unwarranted reaction.

When he was only a few feet behind her stiffly held body, he called her name softly and reached out to grasp her shoulder.

Blair heard him speak her name, and the instant his hand touched her shoulder she spun, dislodging his hand and staring hotly at him. "Enough! I won't be made a fool of any longer."

"I'm sorry, Blair, I really am," Sean said.

Blair gazed at him and saw that he meant what he said. Yet her anger and embarrassment did not lessen.

"It won't happen again, not unless you want it to," Sean promised, his eyes sweeping across her face, taking in the beauty that her tension-filled features could not diminish.

Still Blair said nothing.

Sean shook his head. "What else do you want me to say? Or isn't my apology enough?"

Finally Blair spoke. "It's enough," she whispered.

"Then can we go to our appointment and try and forget what just happened?"

The tension eased but did not leave her completely. Once again Blair found herself changing her mind. "All right."

A few moments later they were in his car and driving along the main street of Narrowsburg. Blair stared straight ahead, her entire body stiff and unyielding as she thought about what had happened. Although she tried to concentrate on what Sean was saying, all she heard were the words he'd already said to her in the restaurant and the truth with which they were laced.

She knew that she was attracted to him, despite her every effort to deny that fact. And she hated herself for her weakness. His very touch sent tendrils of desire throughout her body; one glance from his eyes was enough to make her mind go blank. But she could not give in to him or to her weakness, for Blair knew she would end up hurting too much. And she did not want to be hurt again.

He was right, too, she thought, when he asked her if she had to have a commitment. She was just old-fashioned enough that she could not have an affair. She did need a commitment, just as she'd had with Brian—a commitment that encompassed all things: love, need, desire and above all, a future.

Blair's breath caught when she realized the pathway her mind had led her along. Her thoughts had turned toward a future with Sean.

Blair sat across from Dr. Richard Eldridge, a doctor of psychology and a hypnotherapist. At first glance the slim, gray-haired doctor seemed to be almost too casual in both his dress and his manner of speaking. However, after Blair listened to him for five minutes, she learned what had drawn Sean so deeply into doing this book of reincarnated lovers.

"I know," Dr. Eldridge continued, glancing briefly at Sean, "that I am considered a maverick by my colleagues, but I cannot help doing what I do. Time after time I have regressed patients and have learned of other lives they've lived. I know…" he went on, holding out a hand to ward off any protest, "I know that the current thinking of my professional peers is that the person's mind—the conscious or subconscious—is what develops a fantasy of past lives.

"But as I've told Sean," he said, looking directly into Blair's eyes, "I have found enough proof to satisfy me—which is all the proof of reincarnation I need. The problem is that *he*," Eldridge said, pointing to Sean, "requires hard enough proof to write his book; and I have neither the time nor the inclination to supply all of his requests."

"Yet there is proof enough for you?" Blair asked, speaking for the first time since she was introduced.

"As far as I'm concerned, yes. But from what Sean has told me, that's to be your job. You are the professional researcher who will unearth the facts. You will either prove or disprove my theories."

"If there are facts to be unearthed," Blair agreed.

"There are! Sean has copies of the case histories he is basing his book on. However, they contain only the barest of information—just enough to start you in the right direction." Dr. Eldridge paused to fix Sean with an accusatory stare. "*He* said he wanted it that way."

"That's the way I want to write this book," Sean explained to both Blair and the doctor. "I write all my novels in the same way. I don't see a reason to change my work habits even if this book will be nonfiction. I rough out the basic story without any extra facts or embellishments. In my second draft, I fill in the gaps with my research. That's why I don't want to be encumbered by all the information. Blair will fill in the gaps."

Blair stared at him, her shoulders tense at his explanation. She wondered why he was telling them this story. Willfully Blair shifted her attention from Sean back to the doctor. "Do you have all the things I will need to check on?"

"Absolutely. However, before I give them to you, I would like you to submit to a session of hypnosis."

A sudden warning coursed through Blair's head. "Why?"

"Because I want you to prove that I'm right in my theories. In order to verify what I've discovered, you can't have any doubts about my methods. If you do the research, I believe it's important for you to understand not only where, but how, the original information was gained."

"Can't I listen to the tapes?" Blair asked weakly.

"Of course you can listen to the tapes. I planned on your doing that anyway. But if you're going to do the job, I want you to believe in all the facets of it, not just one."

Nervous at this latest twist of what was fast becoming an overly complicated job, Blair turned to Sean. Without speaking, she used her eyes to ask the question.

"It's up to you," Sean replied, his face devoid of expression.

Blair looked at Dr. Eldridge again. She was fascinated, intrigued and yet uncertain whether she wanted to be hypnotized. "We'll be alone, won't we?" she asked. Sean's quickly stifled laugh echoed in her ears, but she refused to turn and look at him.

Dr. Eldridge smiled sympathetically. "That's just the opposite of what most people ask. They're afraid that I might try to, ah, program them to do strange things. But you're not to worry. Unless the hypnosis is extremely deep—which rarely happens the first time or two—you will remember everything and know what's happening around you at all times."

"I'd still feel safer without Mr. Mathias in the room," Blair stated, making her decision to be hypnotized at the same time.

"No problem," Eldridge said. "Sean, you can pick Mrs. Sanders up in three hours."

"Three hours?" Sean repeated in question, his voice suddenly filled with concern.

Blair stared at him, surprised and not a little touched by his reaction. She was about to say something to him, but Dr. Eldridge spoke first, and with his words, a laugh escaped her lips.

"Are you deaf?" he asked good-naturedly. "I said three hours." Then Eldridge glanced at Blair, who was struggling to contain her first laugh of the day. "Did I say something funny?"

"Yes," Blair replied honestly. "I asked Sean the same question not an hour ago."

Eldridge nodded. "Selective hearing, I would imagine," he declared with a knowing smile.

"Exactly," Blair agreed as she looked at Sean, feeling an unexpected warmth.

"But to put your mind at ease, Sean, the hypnosis session will last only a short while. The rest of the time is for Mrs. Sanders to listen to the regression patients' tapes."

Sean turned to Blair. "In that case I'll be going. I'll pick you up around one. Richard, will you join us for lunch?"

"I wish I could, but I've got a full schedule. Now," Dr. Eldridge said pointedly, "if you'll excuse us?"

With a parting glance at Blair, Sean left, and Dr. Eldridge led Blair to the couch. When she was lying down comfortably, Eldridge began to talk in a calm and reassuring voice.

"What I'm going to do is relatively simple. I'm going to make you relax and then tell you certain things, make certain suggestions. You will do the things I suggest, and you will be aware of doing them. When I bring you back to a fully conscious state of mind, you will remember everything that has happened."

"Are you going to see if I have a past life?" Blair asked a little uncertainly.

Eldridge shook his head. "It's very rare that we can delve that deeply into someone's mind in the first session. No, my only purpose for this session is so you can see that I'm not a charlatan, and for you to understand the state of mind of the patients you'll be researching. That was a part of my understanding with Sean."

"Excuse me?" she asked, confused by his statement. "I don't follow you."

"He didn't tell you?"

"Apparently not," Blair said sarcastically.

"Very commendable. I thought it was an act when you seemed surprised at my request to hypnotize you."

"Would you mind telling me what's going on?" Blair asked without bothering to hide the irritation in her voice.

Dr. Eldridge sat back and nodded. He rested his chin on steepled fingers and gazed at Blair. "I told Sean that if he was to write a book based on my cases, he must be hypnotized before he began work on it. He agreed, but informed me that he always used a researcher for the field work. I told him that I expected the researcher to be hypnotized also. You see," he added as he lowered his hands, "I will not have anyone doing research to disprove my work if they are not familiar with the processes involved."

"I see," Blair said as she tried to digest everything he'd told her. "And Sean? You hypnotized him?"

"Yes, but I can't discuss that." The doctor paused for a moment, and then sighed. "Are you ready?"

Blair nodded, hoping that she would not regret doing this.

"It seems that all we ever do is eat and argue," Blair whispered as she picked at her salad.

"Eating is an important part of life. Arguing is what *you* seem to want to do," Sean replied in a level voice.

Blair stared at him without retorting. They had seemed to declare an uneasy truce to their hostilities, and she did not want to break it.

"What happened when you were hypnotized?" she asked. Watching his face, she saw a startling range of emotions flicker across his once stoic features. But a moment later he smiled.

Sean had been unprepared for Blair's question, and as he gazed at her, he was unable to stop the desires that rose up within him. Holding them back, he smiled secretively. "A lot, but nothing I can discuss with you. You wanted a business relationship, and what happened when I was hypnotized was personal."

"I see," Blair replied tersely. "Well then, do you believe what he's told you?"

"I wouldn't be attempting to write this story if I didn't." Sean paused then to study Blair. His eyes roamed the contours of her face for a moment before he spoke. "Understand something, Blair. Even though I write mostly fiction, if you check any of my facts, you'll find everything is accurate. I've been sued more than once because of my accuracy that some have found unpalatable."

"I know," Blair retorted quickly. "If *you* will remember, I did the research on one of the novels that came under fire," she reminded him.

"So you did," he said, his smile once again in place. "I'm only sorry I didn't meet you then. We wouldn't have wasted a year not knowing each other."

"Sean..." Blair whispered in warning.

"I have to try. What about you? What happened in your session?"

"Nothing. Dr. Eldridge spent a half hour trying to put me under. He said I was too resistant." Blair looked apologetically at Sean before continuing. "However, I did spend the rest of the time listening to the tapes. They couldn't be faked...they were too real."

"Then you believe him?" Sean asked.

"Oh, I believe him," she said, meaning it. "In fact, I can't wait to start the research," she added, unable to mask the excitement filling her voice.

"Now do you understand why I insisted that you come out here before starting the research?"

"Yes," she admitted. Then as casually as she could, she spoke again. "I do have a question I need answered." When she saw him waiting, she held herself back. She did her best to act casual, because she wanted him off guard. When she sensed she'd waited long enough, she began.

"Why did you lie to Dr. Eldridge?"

"What?" Sean asked, surprised at her question.

"No games, Sean. Why did you lie? Alice told me a lot about you, especially the first time I did research for you. She told me the only thing you do before all the research is finished is to write an outline for the publisher. You might be able to fool Dr. Eldridge with what you told him, but, Sean, you can't write a nonfiction book without all the pertinent facts! Why the lie?" she repeated, her tone hard and unrelenting.

Sean saw the challenge in her eyes and in the set of her shoulders. He knew that only the truth would suffice in this instance.

"I lied because Richard has been pestering me for years to write this book. If I told him that I wouldn't start until all the research was finished and in hand, he would have badgered me to no end."

"But he needs you to write it."

Sean shook his head slowly. "It's more than that. After I let him talk me into a hypnosis session and learned what I did, I realized that I wanted to write the book. In fact I had to write it! The lie was my only means of self-defense to give me some peace until I was ready to sit down and write the book."

Blair accepted his words, understanding that the deception practiced on the doctor had indeed been an honest one. "I guess I'm about as ready to start the work as I'll ever be," she commented as she picked through the remains of the salad. "I'll be leaving in the morning. I've been away from the office for too long."

Sean stared at her for several seconds. "Will you have dinner with me tonight?"

Blair knew she should refuse. Her intuition told her just how risky accepting his invitation might be, but in spite of her own common sense, she was becoming lost within the endless depths of his eyes. Without realizing what she was doing, she nodded her answer, and her heart began to beat much too fast.

"Thank you," he whispered.

Chapter Five

Blair drove slowly across the wooden bridge and, when she reached the far side, pulled off the road. The sun was setting as she left the car.

She walked to the edge of the bridge and looked down into the swirling waters of the Delaware. Sighing, she watched the flowing river, only to be reminded of the turbulence within her. Her mind, like the river, was a hard-driving force over which she was losing control.

In an effort to steady her thoughts, Blair lifted her eyes to watch the majesty of the sun's descent behind the high mountains. Suddenly Blair was saddened by the knowledge that she would be leaving this peaceful area in the morning.

Is that all, she asked herself, her thoughts turning introspective. *What about leaving Sean?* But she willed that thought to leave her.

Bending, Blair picked up a twig and thoughtfully studied its chipped bark. Then she released it, consigning it to the water below. She watched the twig twist as it fell, and time stretched infinitely until the twig landed in the river and was carried away. *Is that me? Is that the way I'm reacting to Sean?*

Shrugging because she had no answer, Blair returned to the car and started to drive to Sean's house. Earlier she had called Sean to tell him she would meet him there rather than have him pick her up. By having her car, she would be able to leave whenever she chose, not when he decided.

Turning in at Sean's winding drive, Blair did her best to prepare for the evening ahead. For tonight, she had changed her mode of dress completely. She wore a comfortable pair of jeans that fit perfectly. Her top, a red silky fabric with a crew neck that was open from shoulder to shoulder, fell loosely to her waist. Two small diamond stud earrings sparkled from her earlobes and completed the picture of elegant comfort.

Yet tonight Blair had wanted more than just a change of clothing and had swept the sides of her hair back, using two tortoiseshell combs to secure her hair. Now dry, her layered hair curled out from behind her face to frame it and to show her finely etched cheekbones to perfection, while at the same time accenting her slender neck.

What will happen tonight, she asked herself. *What does he really expect from me?* Blair had spent the better part of the afternoon thinking about Sean and herself. It had been the first time she had actually and consciously allowed her thoughts to run free enough to think in terms of a personal relationship with Sean.

At the same time, she had been brutally honest with herself. Delving within her mind, she had seen that she had been denying all her emotions about him since arriving. Thinking back, she knew she should have realized long before she had that she was more than just mildly attracted to Sean.

Last night's passionate dream was the proof, she told herself. It was, she knew, the confirmation of what she had already discovered about herself. Suddenly, Blair's hands tightened on the steering wheel as yet another truth blossomed within her mind.

Her heart almost stopped under the impact of what she had just learned. "How can that be?" she whispered, once again denying a discovery.

Blair shook her head, but the thought would not leave her. *How could I have fallen in love with him? How?* Then her eyes filled with tears at the enormity and understanding of what had happened.

Oh, Brian, forgive me. I loved you, and I still love you, but I can't deny what I feel any longer. Then Blair shored up her inner strengths and dried her tears. At the same time she made up her mind that she would demand more from Sean than just a fling. She would not be one of his occasional affairs, no matter what the cost or the loss. There must be love on both sides and commitment.

With those thoughts whirling madly in her head, Blair composed herself, shut off the ignition and got out of the car. Walking toward the house, Blair saw a stream of smoke rising skyward from behind the house. When her knock went unanswered, she walked around the side of the house to the back. As she turned the last corner, she saw Sean standing at the barbecue, his back to her, fanning the flames rising from the charcoal.

Unobserved for the moment, she paused to take this opportunity to study him. He too was wearing jeans, and yet another blue shirt, this time a plain T-shirt that stretched enticingly across his back. His waist was slim, and for the first time Blair saw how truly sensuous he was.

Finally, Blair took a deep, anticipatory breath and moved quietly toward him. Deciding to surprise him, she stopped a mere foot from him. Just as she was about to lean forward and cover his eyes with her hands, he spoke.

"Red becomes you."

After dropping Blair off at the motel, where she said she was going to organize her notes from the morning's session with Eldridge, Sean had returned home. Rather than spend the afternoon doing nothing but wondering if Blair would ever admit the way she felt, he'd gone into his study and had begun to put ideas onto paper, writing short, rough outlines of possible future novels.

By six, he stopped so he would have enough time to prepare dinner. After showering and changing into fresh clothing, he took the trout he'd picked up on the way home and set them out. He wrapped two potatoes in foil and put them in the oven, and then cleaned salad greens. While he worked, his thoughts were centered on Blair.

He admitted that his feelings for her were deep and that he could envision a future with her at his side. But, he reasoned, the feelings and emotions had to be two-sided. Although there was an exciting edge in the game they were playing, he wanted it to be over. He wanted to tell her how he felt about her.

If she would only listen to me, he thought. And that, he knew, was half the problem. Blair's defenses were so finely tuned that he doubted whether he could open them wide enough for her to be able to see who he really was. And he was not what she thought him to be. "Far from it," he told the stove as he turned it on.

Sean wasn't a monk, but he wasn't the playboy that his publicity made him out to be either. He dated, but not often, for most women did not like to be shunted aside while he worked. They expected him to stop working at five, like any office person, and be able to devote himself to them.

Sean could not do that. His work governed his personal life. As a writer, his work came from his mind, and he could not shut it off for dinner or a show. When he was working on a novel, there were as many times when he spent twenty straight hours at the typewriter as there were times when he could write only a half page. He had learned that it was a rare woman who could accept the vagaries of his routine.

But he was certain that Blair was one woman who could. *Why,* he asked himself. He had no answer; perhaps it was because he wanted her to.

Sean had no illusions about himself. He knew he was considered handsome, but that was an accident of birth, not something he strove for. He'd also learned early in life to accept what he was and to know his mind and what he wanted. It came as no shock to him that his first sight of Blair had decided his future for him.

As Sean looked around the kitchen, mentally listing the things he would need for that night, he paused again. *What do I have to do to make her stop fighting me as well as herself?*

Sean knew there would be no easy answer to that question, and made himself stop thinking about it and start preparing dinner.

When everything that could be done was done, Sean went outside, set the table on the terrace and then lit the barbecue. As he fanned the flames, his mind again began its twisting journey of conjecture, but suddenly, as he stared into the kitchen window, he saw Blair walking quietly up behind him. Without letting her know he saw her, he watched her come to a stop behind him, and even though he was seeing only a reflection of the real person, he noticed how well her top contrasted with her face.

Just as she leaned forward, he spoke. "Red becomes you."

"How..." Blair started to say as she fought to regain her balance. Before she could steady herself, Sean turned quickly and enfolded her in his arms, cutting off her words with his mouth.

Blair struggled against him, and Sean released her as suddenly as he had taken her in his arms. She stumbled backward, her arms reaching out for support, and just before she could fall, Sean caught her hand and steadied her.

"You promised not to!" she accused him.

"Sorry," he said with a lopsided grin, "it wasn't directed at you, at least not in the way you think. It's an old habit. I always kiss anyone who tries to sneak up on me."

Blair was disarmed by his response. "Anyone?" she asked, picturing Paul Lowery getting kissed by Sean because he'd sneaked up on him.

"Anyone! If it's a man, he won't do it again, will he?" Sean asked, his boyish smile fixed firmly in place.

Blair had the strangest feeling that Sean had read her mind. "How did you know I was behind you?"

"I saw your reflection in the window," he said, cocking his head toward the kitchen window. "The wine is chilling in the ice bucket, and if you're hungry, I'll start dinner now," he informed her with an expression that was a cross between a leer and a grin.

"I'm almost afraid to ask, but what's for dinner?"

"Don't be afraid, Blair," Sean said, his light tones deepening. "Don't ever be afraid." Before she could say or deny anything, Sean smiled again. "Trout," he announced, "with baked potato and spinach salad."

"Sounds wonderful," she said, willing herself to relax after Sean's caution-filled warning. She knew she was treading on thin ice, and her nerves needed to settle down. "Shall I pour the wine?"

"Sure. You didn't ask about dessert."

Blair walked to the table fifteen feet away from the barbecue and lifted the bottle from the chrome bucket. She let the condensed moisture filming the bottle drip back into the bucket before pouring the wine. When the two glasses were at the same level, she replaced the wine in the ice and turned back to him.

"Dessert is fattening."

"Not this dessert," he said with a smile.

"Any dessert is fattening, or worse," Blair said, believing from past experience that he was talking about more than just food.

Once again Sean was aware of her tentative reaction. Then he shook his head sadly. "Stop it, Blair," he said, his voice husky. "It's not a game any longer."

A chill ran along her back as she digested his words. "Sean, I..." Rather than apologize, Blair picked up both wineglasses but still did not move. She looked across the distance that separated them. The power of his unblinking gaze held her in thrall until she felt her throat become as parched as desert sands.

After an eternity of silence, Blair broke free of her trance and walked toward him. Reaching him, she extended a glass, and as he took it, his fingers lingered upon hers for a moment. Another chill raced through her. Then Sean took the glass and raised it in a silent toast before tasting the wine.

Blair returned the toast and let the cool liquid ease the dryness of her throat. A moment later, knowing that she had to break the spell of his eyes, she slowly turned and walked toward the river's edge.

"Did you paint those jeans on?" Sean called to her retreating back. Blair felt a smile build in spite of herself. She didn't turn to answer him; she didn't want him to see the smile. Instead, she shook her head, both in answer and in concession that she couldn't stay serious or mad or anything when he said inane things like that.

"How do you like your fish?" Sean asked, his eyes never leaving her form.

"Cooked," Blair responded, finally turning to look at him. "What other alternatives are there?" she asked with a full smile.

"Substitutions."

"What kind?" Blair asked. The instant the words were out, she realized her mistake.

"Me..."

This time Blair's smile did not disappear; rather, it turned into a wide grin. She had been right about his answer.

Sean was genuinely surprised and puzzled by her smile. He'd tried not to push her. Their last little dialogue had just slipped out. "What are you smiling about?"

"Your predictability," she replied, lifting her wineglass in a salute to him before turning to gaze at the river again.

"It's about time," Sean whispered in a voice he knew would not reach her. Smiling to himself, he felt a weight starting to lift from his shoulders. The first chink in her armor had been opened. *Go slow, don't chase her away now,* he warned himself. And he knew that Blair was too important for him to disregard his own advice.

As soon as the trout was done, Sean called Blair back from the water's edge. After Sean refilled both glasses, they ate on the terrace while the stars winked into existence above them. They finished the meal just as the moon crested a high mountain peak and began to illuminate the ground with silvery light.

"More wine?" Sean asked.

"I think the two glasses I had were sufficient. I've had far too much wine in the past few days."

"Can we talk business?" he asked. He watched as Blair cocked her head to the side and waited for him to continue. "Don't look so wary."

"Who, me?" she asked innocently. "What do I have to be wary of?"

"Nothing," Sean said in a low voice. "Nothing at all. Now," he said in a firmer voice, "the first case you're going to research is Ann Whitten's. She lives in Port Jervis, not far from here. What do you think of her past-life experience?"

Blair thought back to the tapes she'd listened to that morning. She remembered Ann Whitten's clearly. There had been an eerie quality to the woman's voice and an accent and dialect that had sounded like someone's out of the past.

"I think that it will be difficult to get information about her early past life, but easier with the later stages. She supposedly moved to Arizona in 1872 with her father and brothers. They settled on a ranch outside Tuscon. We'll probably find more information in Arizona than New York."

Sean nodded. "My thoughts exactly. When will you go out west?"

"Next week."

"Good. I don't want to rush you, but my editor has informed me that the publisher wants the manuscript as soon as possible. She asked if I could have the first draft ready three months earlier than planned."

"What does that leave me in research time?" Blair asked, mentally working out the amount of time each of the case histories would require.

"A month, six weeks at most."

"Impossible! Not with five case histories!"

"Three weeks for the first two, three weeks for the other three. Blair, I can start the book when the first two people have been researched."

Blair scrutinized his face carefully before speaking. "That's not the way you write," she reminded him. "We've already discussed that. Besides," she continued in a softer voice, "what if I turn something up at the end that needs to be part of the beginning? You'd have to rewrite the entire manuscript."

Sean gazed openly at her, surprised by the emotional response he'd elicited. "You really do care, don't you?"

For a brief moment, his words confused her, but she refused to let the confusion grow. "Of course I do. I want my work to help you, not hold you back. This research is not the norm. If one minor detail crops up later, it can throw the whole thing off."

Sean shook his head. "I'm not talking about the book, Blair, I'm talking about you."

Blair tensed up. She stared openly at him but saw only the deep reflections within his eyes. Suddenly something within her snapped, and her tension and anger faded away. Slowly she nodded her head and sighed. "But that's not the point right now, is it Sean?"

"No," Sean agreed, "I just wanted you to admit it." Then he smiled. "Do you think we might have been lovers in a past life?"

"I hope not!" Blair declared bitterly. She saw Sean's questioning look but was unable to stop the heated flow of her words. "The one thing all the people on Dr. Eldridge's tapes have in common, is that in their past-life experiences they were deeply in love and suffered some great tragedy that lost them their lovers.

"It seems to be a clear pattern with all of them. All of them!" she reiterated. "And I don't want to know that I'd be doomed to repeat a hopeless love over and over again. I'd be content to have just one life and be happy in it." When Blair finished her emotional monologue, a heavy silence wrapped itself around them. She couldn't believe she had opened her mind so quickly to him, and she had certainly not meant to unleash the torrent of emotions that had risen when she spoke.

"That was beautiful," he told her, his features held in serious lines as he took in the moistness filming her eyes. A wave of emotions washed over him at the sight she offered, and he knew that he must break the mood before it turned even heavier. "Coffee?" he asked suddenly.

"Thank you, yes," Blair replied, smiling at him for rescuing her so gallantly from the depths to which her emotions had led her. Her mind was almost a blank after the deeply charged words had been released, and it seemed only a few seconds before Sean returned with two steaming cups of coffee.

"I'll try to have it all done in a month," she said when he sat down. If she used one of her assistants, it just might be possible, she thought.

"Thank you, that would help. By the way, I told my editor that because of the advanced deadline the publisher would have to bear some of the research expense."

"And of course they refused," Blair added, knowing publishers as well as she did.

Sean shook his head. "I'm a best-selling author. If they want a manuscript in early, then they pay the price. They're picking up half the expenses. So, my dear, you can fly first class and charge it directly to Oxworthe Publishing...Blair," Sean began, his voice deepening as he said her name.

Blair tensed. The instant he'd spoken her name, the atmosphere had turned electric, tension filled the air so thickly that she could taste it. His voice sent shivers tumbling along her spine: the way he was gazing at her, his face shadowed from the porch light, took her breath away.

"Blair, don't fight it any longer. I want you...I need you desperately."

Blair's mind reeled with his words. She tried to ignore them, to push them away, but she could not. When she formed her denial, it would not come forth and all she could do was sit silently, her breath tight in her chest, while Sean rose to his full height and came toward her.

His hands reached out and took hers. Slowly, he drew her to her feet. She could not fight him, could not stop him, not here, not now. Blair almost fell against him when his arms encircled her. For the first time in four years, she felt comfortable and protected, yet at the same time totally vulnerable.

Tilting her face, she saw his mouth hovering near hers. His eyes were searching her face even as he lowered his lips.

When their mouths met, Blair's body turned to liquid fire. Her entire being churned with the myriad sensations she had so long repressed. Her breasts, crushed against his chest, welcomed the heat radiating from his body. Her hands were on his back now, her fingers could feel his every movement through the thin fabric of his shirt. Her thighs pressed closely to his. And in that special place deep within her a yearning, long-unfelt desire grew.

When Sean's mouth left hers, she gasped; when his mouth returned, an involuntary cry of pleasure sprang from her mouth as his lips covered the sensitive skin on her neck. The all-consuming and fiery trail that blazed from just below her ear to her collarbone sent her mind spinning. He shifted, and as he did, Blair realized that his hand was caressing her breast. Her sharp intake of breath was accompanied by the instant stiffening of her nipple. Pulsing electric shocks went from the palm of his hand into her breast. Then his hand was gone and she was being lifted. With her eyes closed and her head against his chest, Blair allowed Sean to carry her off.

Slowly, the knowledge of what was about to happen filled her mind. Burying her face into his lean, hard chest, she forced her voice to work. "Please, Sean, not yet," she whispered, fighting to control the desires that contradicted every word she'd spoken.

"Shhh, don't say anything else," Sean told her in a husky, desire-filled voice as he walked a short distance from the porch and set Blair down upon a velvet cushion of grass.

Lulled by his voice and the warmth of the night, Blair opened her eyes. Gazing up at him, her mouth dry, her body aching with need for him, she did not speak again.

Sean knelt beside her, his eyes devouring the beauty of her face for several seconds before he kissed her again and tasted the warm sweetness that seemed always a part of her lips.

Blair's resistance was weakened by the gentle insistence of his lips upon hers, and even when his hand freed her top from the confines of the jeans, she could not stop him. When his fingers moved in slow and lazy circles on her stomach, her skin began to glow with desire.

Blair knew she was fast losing her ability to stop what was happening, but her mind was no longer able to fight against her heart's command to let herself free. Slowly, tantalizingly, Sean's hand rose along her abdomen until it slipped beneath the silky fabric of her bra to cup one tender breast. Blair's back arched; her low moan floated toward the stars.

"I need you, Blair," Sean whispered, his voice laden with passion as he took one of her delicate earlobes between his teeth.

Blair raised her arms, her hands going to his head, her fingers weaving through his smooth black hair. A moment later her fingers entwined deeply into his hair and drew his face to her. She kissed him deeply, their tongues dancing in tune with their passions. A foggy memory of the previous night's dream impinged on her mind as the reality of what was happening grew within her consciousness, but everything had an ethereal quality that she could no longer fight against.

The need to see him, to gaze at his handsome features and drink in their masculine beauty filled her, and Blair opened her eyes. Her hands were still lodged in his hair; she slowly released him while letting her fingertips explore the lines of his face. In that moment, the kiss ended and he drew slightly away from her.

As her fingers traced his cheeks, her wedding band glinted beneath the soft glow of the moon. An icy chill slashed through Blair's mind, instantly cooling her molten desires. She stared wide-eyed at the ring, oblivious of anything else in the world, paralyzed and trapped by her past.

A torrent of memories overwhelmed her, and she was so caught by what flashed before her eyes that she did not feel Sean pull away from her. Then, with a sudden crystal clarity she had never known before in her life, Blair saw the truth of who and what she was.

Brian was gone from her. Her life and her destiny were again under her own guidance. She also realized that her love for Brian was special and would always remain so; but it would not prevent her from loving and being loved again.

When Sean had felt Blair stiffen against him, he had drawn back from her. Desire and need coursed through his veins, sped along by his emotions. But as he gazed at her, he too froze. Her eyes were wide and staring, not at him, but at the wedding band on her left hand. In that instant a curtain of anger descended to block his need and love for Blair as he realized exactly what she was doing.

His hand, still on her breast, could feel the rapid rise and fall of her breathing, but her skin no longer warmed his palm. Slowly he withdrew his hand and leaned farther away from her.

Blinking her eyes to free herself, Blair belatedly realized that Sean had pulled away from her and was staring at her in stiff disbelief, his chiseled features held immobile. Suddenly, Blair understood the look he was favoring her with, for disgust and loathing were fully etched upon his features.

Blair shook her head. "Sean," she called in a hoarse whisper, "It's not...it's not what you think."

"Don't make excuses," he snapped, his voice constricted by hurt. "I think you found the perfect way to save your virtue. Just perfect!" His voice never rose above a whisper, but to Blair it was as loud as a cannon.

Then Sean stood to tower above her shaken form. His face was still hard, and his words when he spoke dropped with accusation. "Just perfect!" he repeated. "You let a man begin to make love to you and then when he's almost beyond control with his need for you, you look at your wedding band and pretend that your husband has come back to you!"

The cruelty of his words stabbed at Blair like knives slashing across her body. But she knew that she must find some way to make him understand what had happened. "You're wrong Sean. It isn't like that at all. It was—" But before she could finish her explanation, Sean broke into her words.

"I'm not interested in what you have to say. Your actions spoke eloquently enough. I was wrong! I should have accepted you for what you said you were and not allowed my needs to influence my mind!"

Blair heard the deep, ragged breath that Sean took when he finished his tirade. She had never felt more helpless before. Then the anger and hurt that had covered his features while he spoke disappeared, and in their place was an expression that showed nothing—not even the contempt she had heard in his voice.

Blair's mind went numb. The soaring passions of moments ago; her newfound understanding that she did have a life of her own; the scorn Sean had shown her—these became too much for her to bear. But before she could even move, Sean spoke again.

"Blair," he said in a monotone, "you have my word that from this moment on the only thing we will share is work. I will not give you a repeat performance of these past days." With that, he turned and started toward the porch.

Blair stayed motionless on the grass, too stunned to move. Her body was still drugged by the passions she'd felt, and her mind and heart too hurt to force herself to move. She watched him, feeling as though she were part of an audience in a movie, while Sean cleared the table they had shared a short time before and took the dishes inside.

Finally, Blair struggled to a sitting position. She was confused and felt foolish and even more vulnerable than she had earlier in Sean's arms. But as she tried to form some order within her thoughts, anger slowly emerged.

I'm a grown woman, she told herself. *I was married, and am a success in my profession. Why am I acting like a virginal little girl?* Her anger was directed not at Sean but at herself, and it gave her the strength to do what she must. And what she needed to do was to talk to Sean and straighten out this misunderstanding before the chasm became too wide to cross.

Forcing life into her resistant legs, Blair stood. After straightening her top and tucking it neatly into her waistband, she started toward the porch. As soon as Sean reappeared, Blair went over to him.

"Sean, I want to explain what happened." When Sean turned to face her, she saw his features were devoid of expression; his eyes were hard and unrelenting.

"No, Blair, I think your actions were explanation enough. I was the one who made the mistake, not you. You're still in love with your husband, and I can't compete with a memory." For just an instant, Sean felt his hard-held mark slip, but he recovered quickly. "But I will ask for your forgiveness for my outburst. It was cruel and unnecessary, and I am sorry. Now, I think it best if you leave."

Blair's anger grew swiftly, but her humiliation blanketed it. Heat rose to her cheeks, and she intuitively knew that no matter what she said to him he would not listen. Finally, it was her own pride that would not allow her to make any further explanations.

"Very well," she said stiffly, "I'll call you when I've finished the first report." With that, Blair turned and left. She walked slowly, refusing to run away from him, and forced her back to stay straight and not show the suffering that attacked her so fiercely. Once in the car, Blair started it and drove recklessly out of the driveway, slewing the car sideways when she turned onto the main road.

Suddenly, unable to control her emotions any longer, Blair jammed on the brakes. When the car stopped, amid the protesting squeal of tires, she let her head drop to the steering wheel as her tears began to flow.

Chapter Six

The moon was falling behind the mountains as Sean stood on the bank of the Delaware. He'd been there for several hours, working to sort out the turmoil of his feelings and trying his damnedest to convince himself that Blair Sanders didn't matter to him. But in the fading hours of the night, long after Blair had gone, he could not make himself believe his thoughts. Instead, he was beginning to accept the possibility that he might have made a mistake.

Sean wondered why he had not let her explain herself, and realized that he had been wrong not to let her. He could picture her face as she had tried to speak to him, and saw again the deep hurt etched upon her delicate features. The moistness of her eyes when he'd condemned her had stayed with him since the moment she'd left.

"Damn it all!" he shouted to the star-filled sky. Turning, Sean walked, not to the house, but to the low-slung sports car sitting in the drive. An instant later the peaceful night was shattered by the growl of the engine and the shriek of tires on macadam.

Seven minutes later, Sean pulled to a stop in front of Blair's motel room. Leaving the car, Sean was determined to talk to her and find out what had really happened. There was no more room for games.

He knocked on the door and waited. A minute later, he knocked again, louder. When there was still no answer, Sean turned from the door and noticed what he had failed to before. Blair's car was not in the parking lot.

Turning back to the door, Sean tried the knob. The door swung open and he went inside. The moment he flicked on the lights, he knew he was too late. Blair was gone.

Blair stared out her office window. She would have preferred a better view, say Central Park, but the rent for this office made the view bearable. The offices of Sanders Research occupied the third floor of a converted town house on Fifty-third Street, and Blair was watching the people who milled on the busy sidewalk below.

She knew it might be her last chance to look at familiar things for several weeks, and she wanted to drink her fill of it all. Blair's assistant, Laura, had already made all the flight reservations for her. The first leg of the research trip was to Arizona, and from there to California. After California she would go to Mexico City.

At that point, and depending on how much time she had spent, Blair would decide if there was enough time left for her to complete the research herself. If not, she would send Laura to Tennessee and Stephanie, her other assistant, to Boston.

Blair's intercom buzzed, interrupting her thoughts. Sighing, she turned back to her desk and flicked the switch. "Yes?"

"Alice Daniels to see you," Laura announced. Blair stiffened. She hadn't spoken to Alice and had avoided all her friend's calls since arriving home on Sunday. It was now Tuesday afternoon and Blair had hoped to be on the seven-thirty flight that evening without having to see or talk to her.

Blair knew herself well enough to know that she might not be able to control her anger and she was afraid that until she settled her own thoughts, she did not want to risk hurting her long-standing friendship with Alice. Three weeks should give her enough time to cool her thoughts about Alice's indiscretion with Sean.

"Send her in," Blair reluctantly instructed Laura.

When the office door opened, Alice Daniels walked in. Blair noted that Alice looked as chic as ever with her tall, model's good looks. Today was Dior, one of the designer's more conservative suits of gray velvet. A pink silk blouse nestled beneath the expensively cut jacket, and a small black string tie pulled the entire look together. Alice's blonde waves bounced softly as she went over to Blair, who had risen to meet her halfway.

"My goodness, Blair, trying to see you is harder than getting an appointment with the President," Alice commented after kissing Blair on the cheek.

"I've been busy," Blair replied, and was immediately distressed at the coolness of her voice.

"I know, I made you that way. Listen, love, we need to chat before you leave on this trip."

"Alice, could it wait until I get back?" Blair asked, forcing her voice to stay light.

"I don't think I want to wait three weeks. Really, Blair, it's important," Alice stated as she sat on the small love seat across from Blair's desk.

Suddenly, Blair's control slipped and her anger broke through. She walked over to her friend and stood above her, arms akimbo. "I'm sure it is important. What do you need? More information to pass on to other people? Who will it be this time?" Blair asked, biting off each word.

Alice tensed and her perfectly arched eyebrows rose slightly before resettling into place. For an instant, a small grin played at the corner of her mouth. "Ease off," she said.

"Don't give me orders! I'm well aware of how much I owe you. If it wasn't for you, I'd probably still be sitting behind a locked door with my drapes closed. But all you've done for me still does not give you the right to spew my life history to any male you feel inclined to violate my trust to." Blair's breath was ragged with anger; her mind was raging, and she no longer cared what the results of her words would be on their friendship.

"Finished?" Alice asked calmly.

Blair could not believe her friend was as unruffled as she appeared. "No!" Blair spat. "I was almost seduced, and I made a complete fool out of myself, and there's only one person to blame.... You!"

"Finished?"

"I can stop there if you want," Blair retorted sarcastically.

"Please," Alice said with a smile and wave of her hand, "go on and finish."

"Stop smiling. I'm mad as hell at you. You're supposed to be my friend. I relied on you for more than I should have, but you were always there. I trusted you with my deepest thoughts; I poured my heart out to you. And you repaid my trust by telling the world about my private life."

"I don't think telling one person is the same as telling the world."

"Don't play the innocent with me. One person or a hundred, what's the difference?" Blair demanded.

"Sit down next to me," Alice said, patting the cushion next to her.

Blair shook her head defiantly, her eyes still glowering.

"Please," Alice asked.

Blair sighed and went to the love seat. Sitting, she half turned to face Alice.

"Blair, I love you like the sister I never had. We've been friends since high school. Do you really think I'd break a confidence if I didn't think I was doing the right thing?"

"But it wasn't the right thing," Blair protested, but as she did, her anger began to fade.

"Listen, hon, Sean Mathias is very taken with you. I didn't even realize he'd met you until he started badgering me about you. And, Blair, I know him. He's a sweet, sensitive and wonderful man. I don't know what happened when you two got together, but I think you should tell me."

Blair laughed bitterly. "I can't believe Sean hasn't told you yet. I was positive he'd enjoy relating all the sordid details."

"I don't understand. I think you're talking about a different Sean Mathias from the one I know. Are you sure that it was Sean you met in upstate New York?" Alice asked, a puzzled expression spreading across her face.

"Of course it was Sean. When did he start badgering you about me?" she asked suddenly.

"A half hour after you left the party," Alice responded, not the least put off by Blair's change in direction. "Blair, what happened?"

Blair looked at Alice and felt tears begin to rise. *No!* she commanded herself, *I will not weaken again.* Blair had not permitted herself to cry since that night on the road near Sean's house. When she'd finally gotten herself under control, she had driven slowly back to the motel, packed her bag and checked out. Then, as tired as she was, she'd driven back to New York City and to the comfort and safety of her apartment. By the time she'd reached home, Blair had vowed never to allow another man to get as close to her as Sean had.

But sitting across from her dearest friend, and after venting all her pent-up anger, she could not stop the tears from spilling out. When Alice's arms went around her and Alice drew her to her bosom, she let the tears fall until there were no more to shed. Finally, she wiped her eyes with the back of her hand and smiled tentatively at Alice.

"Your jacket...I'm sorry," Blair said, staring at the large wet spot her tears had created.

"Salt water is good for velvet," Alice replied with a smile.

"And I'm sorry for blowing up at you. But...you deserved it," she added defensively.

"I still want to know what happened to make you so angry," Alice insisted.

Blair studied her friend for a moment and then felt the need to talk rise within her. And talk she did. For almost an hour the words poured forth. She told Alice everything that had happened, sparing nothing, not even her final humiliation at the end. When she finished, she sighed.

"So you're in love with him. Lovers always have quarrels," Alice stated.

"It doesn't matter. I won't be one of his cast-off affairs. I won't be used until he grows tired of me and goes after his next conquest."

Alice's laugh caught Blair off guard. She shook her head slowly. "I still think you met the wrong person."

"Alice," Blair cried in frustration. "He's a ladies' man. We both know that. The whole world knows that. Pick up any paper and look in the gossip column."

"Come on, sweetie, you know that publicity sells books."

"I will not be a part of that type of publicity."

"Sometimes, Blair Sanders, you're so thick I just want to bang your head against a wall. Sean is in love with you!" Alice stated.

"Don't give me...Sean is what?" Blair demanded, not believing her ears.

"I said he's in love with you," Alice repeated.

Blair stared at her with accusation flowing from her eyes. "I thought you said he didn't tell you what happened?"

"I haven't spoken to Sean since the day before you left him. He told me then."

Blair thought her brain had turned into a crossword puzzle and she was supposed to fill in the missing words. "He never met me before I went upstate."

"Yes, he did, at the party. Blair, after Sean convinced me to tell him about you, he told me about himself. He said that the moment he saw you he fell in love with you."

"Oh, please," Blair said with a shake of her head.

"It's the truth, damn it!" Alice snapped, losing her composure for the first time. "He felt so strongly about you that he told me he was going to your office the next morning and tell you how he felt. I convinced him that that would not work." Alice paused to shake her head.

"That's when he said he would wait until you started working on the reincarnation research before sweeping you off your feet and into his life."

"You mean his bed, don't you?"

"That's part of his life," Alice retorted quickly. "Blair, I'm sorry for what happened, I really am."

"That doesn't make it any easier," Blair said in a whisper, half-smiling at Alice to show her words were not said in anger.

"No, it doesn't, but at least you know more than you did before."

"Why didn't you warn me?"

"I couldn't."

"Why? Would Sean have left you for another agent?"

"Hardly. He knows he couldn't get a better agent."

"Then why?"

Alice took one of Blair's hands and held it tightly. "Because if I had told you, you wouldn't have gone. And then neither of you would have fallen in love. And besides, Sean does need you to do the research. There's no one better."

"Thanks for the compliment," Blair said dryly, "but I didn't need to fall in love again. Once was enough. Now I've lost twice," Blair said sadly.

"You haven't lost Sean," Alice told her. "It's not too late."

"It is for me. It just hurts too much. Alice, I don't want to be in love with Sean Mathias. I'll finish this job and then I'll be free of him forever."

"Forever is a long time," Alice warned.

"Is it? The research I'm doing says it may not be as long as we think."

"Blair!" Alice snapped in exasperation. But the intercom's buzzing interrupted whatever she was about to say.

Rising swiftly, Blair went to the desk and flipped the switch. "Yes?"

"Shall I call the cab? You have to be at Kennedy Airport in an hour."

Blair looked at her small quartz desk clock and realized how long she'd been talking with Alice.

"You'd better call, and thank you, Laura," Blair said before turning back to Alice. "I'm glad you came. If I'd put this talk off until I got back, I probably wouldn't have been able to even say hello to you."

"Besides confiding to, and laughing with, friends are for yelling at also," Alice said philosophically. "Let me go to the airport with you, and we'll have a drink to send you on your way."

"No date tonight?" Blair asked coyly.

"Only you."

Blair smiled. "I'd love the company," she admitted as she walked to the closet, opened it and took out two suitcases. "I hope these will be enough for three weeks."

"Blair," Alice called in a low voice.

Blair sensed what Alice was about to say and stopped her quickly. "No more today, please."

"Only one more thing. While you're gone, would you think about what I said?"

Blair stared at Alice and slowly nodded. In her mind, Blair knew that she had no choice about whether she would or would not think of Sean—none.

Blair stretched languorously on the oversize bed. The soft hum of the air conditioner was the first sound she became aware of. Glancing around, Blair smiled as she looked at the clock on the bed table. Ten o'clock.

Yawning once, Blair sat up. She left the bed and padded across the deep carpeting to the ornate bathroom and once inside turned on the shower. After brushing her teeth, Blair stepped beneath the cascading water.

Ten minutes later, clad only in a short terry robe, she stepped out onto the balcony, thirty-two stories above Mexico City.

The tropical sun, already a hotly burning disk, warmed her quickly. Blair ran her fingers through her layered hair to help the sun dry it. When her eyes drifted downward, she suddenly grasped the railing for support as a wave of vertigo swept through her. Forcing herself to take several deep breaths, she willed the dizziness away and began to appreciate the view.

Mexico City sprawled out beneath her. The multicolored roofs of the old homes mixed with the modern structures of the city to present a tableau that was both exotic and beautiful.

Church bells pealed through the air, calling the city's inhabitants to their various services. Throngs of people in brightly shaded clothing walked the streets while others gathered in small parks and plazas.

I am glad I changed my plans, Blair thought. A deep and satisfying sense of a job well done settled in her mind.

With a sigh that encompassed relief and tiredness, Blair thought about her trip. She'd just finished ten nonstop days of working herself close to exhaustion. But her feeling of accomplishment made it seem worthwhile.

Blair had not once forgotten her promise to try to finish the research within a month. And she knew she had a good chance of doing just that. Tomorrow, Monday, she would start the research on her third subject. The first two had taken her only the ten days preceding her arrival in Mexico.

"Yes," Blair said to the city below, "tomorrow." When she had changed her plans at the last minute and switched her flight from California so that she could arrive the previous night, she had wondered if it had been a wise move, because there would be no work done in Mexico on a Sunday.

At the same time Blair had known that she needed to get a day's rest, and flying in that day would have denied her that rest. Smiling, Blair knew that all she would do today would be lie in the sun and relax, and let all the things she'd learned in the past days be absorbed by her mind.

Turning, Blair retreated into the coolness of the room. The room, one of the better ones at the prestigious El Castile, was large, spacious and ultramodern. *Too modern,* Blair thought, but conversely, it was perfectly bland and would allow her to concentrate on her work.

Blair went to the dresser and took out a tank-style pale lavender bathing suit. She put on the form-hugging suit, which had a single strap crossing one shoulder.

Glancing in the mirror, Blair nodded to herself, pleased by the gentle look of lavender against her paler skin. She took her light robe rather than a pullover top and, after slipping into her sandals, scooped up her purse and started for the door.

Before opening the door, she paused to glance back over her shoulder. Looking at her leather attaché case, she felt a tendril of guilt grow in her mind. She shook away the feeling in favor of the relaxation she'd promised herself. She would have a light breakfast, Blair decided, before claiming a lounge by the pool.

It was almost two o'clock when Sean finished unpacking his suitcase. He took a small leather traveling kit and put it on the bathroom counter. After opening it, he stared at its contents and shook his head. Then he looked at his reflection on the bathroom mirror.

"You've done some strange things in your time," he told his image, "but I think this one will top them all."

Shaking his head, Sean left the bathroom. He began to pace slowly, trying to discharge the restless energy building within him. Ten minutes later he changed into his bathing suit and went downstairs. He stopped in the hotel's lobby to hand the desk clerk a note before continuing on to the pool.

Once there, he put on sunglasses and a hat and then looked around cautiously. Finally, he picked a spot and settled himself in a lounge chair.

Blair moved out of the intense heat of the afternoon sun to a cooler spot beneath a large floral-print umbrella. She knew the limits of her susceptibility to the sun and did not want to get burned. A few minutes after she sat on the lounge chair, a deeply tanned pool boy came over to inquire if she wanted a drink. Blair ordered a piña colada. Five minutes later she was sipping the frozen pineapple-coconut drink through a cutoff straw and sighing with pleasure as the icy coolness of the drink went slowly toward her stomach.

She started to close her eyes but opened them quickly. She had not liked what she had seen imprinted on the back of her lids. For it was Sean Mathias's taunting smile, deep eyes and smooth jet hair that had materialized, unbidden.

A little of the joy of her personal day disappeared as Blair tried to force his image away. And she had no choice but to admit that the real reason she had pushed herself so hard since leaving New York was not so much to get the job completed quickly as it was to help her forget Sean. She had pushed herself mercilessly from early morning to late at night so that she would be too tired to think. She wanted to be incapable of remembering the way his lips had felt on hers and the way his arms had held her so securely. She had not wanted to think of the passions that he brought out in her or of the need she had for him. Blair knew that work was her only salvation; only work could rid her of his haunting visage.

Blair had also come to the conclusion that there was no possible future for them—no matter what Alice had told her. She'd realized that when she'd spoken to him from Arizona after finishing the first step in her research.

Sean had been cool and businesslike. Too cool. The second time she'd called him, three days ago from Santa Barbara, he'd sounded the same. *No,* Blair reminded herself, he'd sounded even more distant than before.

Forget him, he doesn't want you, she told herself, *at least not the way you want him. It wouldn't have worked anyway,* Blair added to her silent inner dialogue.

Yet she could not rid herself of the picture that Alice had drawn of Sean that last day in New York. Alice had described a man whom she'd never met. But Blair also remembered the strange conversation she'd had with Erica Lowery. And Erica's words were too similar to Alice's to be ignored.

But why do I see him so differently? Then Blair realized that all her tortured thoughts were being wasted, for even if Sean had indeed loved her, what had happened on the lawn their last night together had destroyed any feelings that Sean might have for her.

Blair decided then and there that she would not risk making a fool of herself again. She would forget Sean, she had to.

Lifting the almost forgotten glass to her mouth, Blair captured the straw and drew out more of the frozen drink as her eyes wandered around the pool area. Many guests were enjoying the sun and the luxurious facilities of the hotel. People of every culture were there, and the variety of skin colors and hair colors, sizes and shapes, presented a kaleidoscope of the world's populace. Near her she heard three slender Frenchmen talking to two tall, statuesque Scandinavian-looking women.

Blair's eyes skimmed past a man wearing a hat and a blue bathing suit, stopped and quickly returned to him. She felt a shock of recognition when she studied the smoothly muscled back. *No, it can't be him,* she told herself, cursing her eyes for playing tricks on her.

Sighing, Blair picked up the novel she had been attempting to read ever since her plane had left California. She tried valiantly to concentrate, but after a few minutes she gave up, unable to resist the urge to look at the man again. Glancing over the top of the book, she sought him out. The chair he'd been in was empty. Blair looked around quickly and saw the man entering an archway across from her. At the flash of blue from his bathing suit, Blair realized her mistake. It had been the blue bathing suit, not the man, that had caught her eyes. Sean always wore blue. *It's not him,* she told herself, understanding that it had been her own deceptive mind that made her think it was Sean.

Returning to the novel, Blair started to read again. Slowly, without realizing what was happening, her eyelids grew heavy. Soon her work-tired body conspired with her emotionally exhausted mind to lull Blair to sleep on the lounge.

A gentle but insistent shaking on her shoulder woke Blair. Opening her eyes slowly, Blair saw the tanned pool boy who had brought her drink standing over her.

"Six o'clock, Senorita, the pool is closing," he told her in a lightly accented voice.

"Gracias," Blair replied as she sat up.

"De nada," the pool boy rejoined with a smile as he turned away and began to pick up the discarded towels that littered the pool area.

Standing, Blair stretched and put on her robe. Then she went to the archway that wound through the gardens and led to the lobby. She inhaled the mixed fragrances of tropical blossoms and smiled at the beautifully flamboyant plants. Once she entered the air-conditioned lobby, she went to the desk to see if there were any messages.

She immediately noticed a white sheet in her room box and asked the clerk for it. When he handed it to her, she glanced quickly at it and her heart skipped a beat. Sean had called, the message said, and he would call her back at seven-thirty.

Why was he calling, she wondered. *Had something come up concerning the research?* Blair's mind was so busy, as she entered the waiting elevator, that she didn't remember pressing her floor button. When she heard the elevator's chime and looked up, she found herself on the thirty-second floor.

Walking absently to her room, she unlocked the door and went in. Once inside, she shook her head to clear away the questioning thoughts and dropped her purse on the dresser.

She turned then and from the corner of her eye saw a rainbow of colors. Blinking, Blair realized the colors were a bouquet of tropical flowers rising out of a glass vase that sat upon the small coffee table separating two upholstered chairs.

Her breath caught as she lifted a small white envelope and opened it.

> *Thank you for working so hard*
> *Sean*

"Why?" she asked the flowers. Shrugging helplessly, Blair turned away and began to undress. She looked at the clock, saw she had an hour before Sean would call and decided to take a bath.

At the doorway to the bathroom, she turned to look at the flowers. Her eyes misted and emotions welled up strongly within her.

"It's not fair," she whispered. "You're not fair," she whispered again at Sean's image.

Chapter Seven

At exactly seven-thirty Blair's telephone rang. Although she was expecting the call, the shattering of the quiet of the room made her jump. She forced herself to let the phone ring three times before she picked it up, and when she did, she found herself straining to keep her voice level.

"Enjoying yourself?" Sean asked in a pleasantly modulated voice.

"Yes, thank you. And...thank you for the flowers."

"It was my pleasure. I hope you weren't working today."

"No, I decided to treat myself to a day off, but I fell asleep by the pool," she said.

"You didn't get burned, did you?" Sean asked.

Blair thought she detected concern in his voice. "No, I was under an umbrella."

"Good, I wouldn't want you out of commission, especially at the rate you're going."

Anger was Blair's first response to his words. She fought to keep her voice level, but did not quite succeed. "You don't have to worry, I know how to take care of myself," she informed him in stiff tones.

"I know you do, Blair, I know you do."

"Sean," she said a moment later, her voice once again under control, "are you calling about the research?"

"No," he said.

Blair held the phone tightly, her heart racing while she waited for him to continue. When he did not, she spoke again. "Why did you call?"

"A very close friend of mine is staying at your hotel. When I spoke to him, I told him you were doing some research for me. He's a fellow writer, and told me to have you meet him so that he could show you around. He's very familiar with Mexico City."

"I don't need a guide for what I have to do. I'm fluent in Spanish, and I can find my own way," she stated coolly.

"Blair, I've already told him that I would arrange for him to meet you. He's a very nice man, and more importantly, he could be a valuable business contact."

When Sean grew silent, Blair listened to the static in the receiver while she thought about that he'd said. "Please," was Sean's next word.

Blair sighed in resignation. "All right."

"Good. He's reserved a table in the hotel's dining room for nine o'clock. His name is Ronald Herman."

"Reserved a table? I said I would meet him, not have dinner with him, and not tonight.... Ronald Herman, the science fiction writer?" she asked a moment later.

"The same. You've read his work?" Sean asked.

Blair smiled into the receiver. "I've always been something of a science-fiction fan," she admitted. "I love the way he writes. Ronald Herman is one of my favorites among the new writers."

"Then you'll have dinner with him?" Sean asked.

"I don't know.... I wish you hadn't arranged for dinner."

"It won't hurt you to relax," Sean coaxed. "Besides, I thought that after ten days of traveling in unfamiliar places you might enjoy spending time with someone you had something in common with."

"I don't know the man. What would we have in common?"

"You're both in the same field—publishing."

Blair sighed at the futility of the argument. "All right, Sean."

"Wonderful. By the way, how long do you think you'll be in Mexico?"

"I don't know yet. I'll have a better idea tomorrow after I've gone to the library," she replied.

"Fine, keep in touch."

"I will," Blair promised as she heard the click of his telephone. "Goodbye," she whispered to the broken connection.

Only after she hung up did Blair realize that she had spent ten minutes on the phone with Sean, and he had been warm, charming and close. The coolness and distance she had felt in the other calls had been absent tonight.

"Damn him!" she shouted to the flowers. "Why is he doing this to me?" Standing, Blair wondered what she should wear for dinner with the famous Ronald Herman.

Blair had read all five of Ronald Herman's novels, including the one that had won science-fiction's highest award, and she realized that she could not remember ever having seen his photo. As she recalled what she knew about the writer, several important facts came to mind.

Unlike many authors, Ronald Herman was publicity shy. It was rumored that he was a recluse, avoiding newspeople and fans alike. He never granted interviews to any publication except science-fiction magazines, not even after winning science fiction's highest award, and had never allowed his picture to be placed on a book jacket. The rare interviews he did give to the sci-fi magazines were always conducted via telephone.

Nodding to herself at her memory of the author, Blair realized that tonight would indeed be a rare privilege. Then Blair went to the closet and looked over her clothing. She knew what she had brought with her but thought that looking over the dresses would help her decide which one to wear. As she searched, she began to wonder what Ronald Herman would be like. Hopefully, nothing like Sean.

Suddenly Blair was uncertain about the wisdom of her decision to have dinner with the writer, even if it did mean more business for her.

Lifting out a burgundy cocktail dress, Blair inspected it critically. *It will do,* she decided.

Sean hung up the telephone and smiled. The first part of his plan had worked. "Now for the tricky part," he murmured. Standing, he went into the large bathroom of his room in the El Castile, which just happened to be the room adjoining Blair's.

Being a celebrity does have its advantages, he told himself. *And its drawbacks,* he added.

In the bathroom he withdrew several items from the leather case that he'd placed on the counter earlier. Working carefully, and remembering the exact way he had described what he was about to do in one of his novels, he applied a light coat of glue to his chin, working the brush upward toward his sideburns.

He repeated the procedure with his eyebrows. After letting the adhesive dry to the proper tackiness, he applied one eyebrow and then the other. When they were attached, he lifted up a jet-black swatch of hair that remained and carefully placed it on his face. A moment later, he smoothed it along his skin, separating it at his mouth.

When Sean stepped back, he looked at himself critically in the mirror. The bearded face was foreign to him and not at all bad looking, he decided.

"How long will it take her to see through this?" he asked his image.

Then he shook his head slowly. He felt almost foolish for going to this length, but whenever he'd tried to say something to Blair in their two phone calls, the chilly sound of her voice had stopped him before he could start.

When he'd talked to Alice and told her that it was over before it had begun, Alice had refused to listen to him. She wouldn't say why. All she would say was that he shouldn't give up without a fight no matter what had already happened.

But Sean knew it wasn't Alice's words that had made him decide to face Blair. It was his own driving emotions that would not permit him to give up.

Still, he knew that if he were to just walk up to her, here in Mexico City, she would run away from him. He needed to make her listen to what he had to say, and he was willing to do whatever was necessary to achieve his goal.

Perhaps I'm going a little too far, he told himself as he studied his Ronald Herman face. Then he smiled, thinking that he should have done this six years ago when he'd received the award, instead of insisting on anonymity. But he had needed to protect his pseudonym. He had wanted his science-fiction novels—which for Sean were philosophically speculative novels rather than pure science fiction—to stand on their own merit and not be judged by his popular fiction writing. Only Alice Daniels, he and his sci-fi editor knew that Sean Mathias and Ronald Herman were one and the same person.

"All right, Blair, this is it. Tonight we work it out."

Blair walked through the elegant hotel lobby toward the dining room. The sounds of multilingual conversations filled the air, accompanied by mariachi music escaping from the lounge. In all, the atmosphere in the hotel was one of excitement. The night life of Mexico City was just beginning, and Blair wondered just how much a part of it she would be.

Passing a mirrored wall, Blair took a quick glance at herself. The burgundy cocktail dress looked good on her; its scooped neck showed just a hint of cleavage while at the same time its form-fitting bodice outlined her well-proportioned figure with just the right amount of propriety.

Black leather open-toed shoes matched the clutch in her right hand, and as usual Blair wore a minimum of jewelry. Two small gold hoop earrings and a thin, lightweight gold chain completed the look.

Tonight she had changed her hairstyle again, this time sweeping one side back and using a hairpin to secure a small flower from the bouquet Sean had sent to her hair.

At the dining-room entrance, Blair bypassed the line of waiting people and went directly to the front in search of the maître d'. While she waited for him, she glanced at the interior of the dining room. It was softly lit, almost dark, with tables placed in a seemingly random pattern. The walls held paintings illuminated by hidden spotlights in the ceiling.

The room itself was alive with both diners and the people who served them. Romantic music came from the rear, and Blair saw a trio of musicians playing stringed instruments. The aromas wafting through the air assailed her senses. Rich spices, mingling with the scents of meat, fish and fowl, made her mouth water. As Blair took in everything, she never stopped searching for a table that held but one occupant.

"May I help you, senorita?" came the voice of the maître d'. Turning, Blair found herself face to face with a man of her own height, whose dark hair and thin mustache were set off nicely by an elegant black tuxedo.

"Thank you. I am meeting Mr. Herman for dinner."

"Ah, yes, *Senora* Sanders," he said with a smile. "This way please." The maître d' motioned gallantly with his arm as he escorted Blair to Ronald Herman's table. Blair followed him in the semidarkness as he maneuvered between the tables and then turned a corner to enter a smaller, alcovelike room off the main dining room. This room held only tables for two. Finally, the maître d' stopped at a table in one corner and held out a chair for her.

There was no candle on this table, and Blair could barely see the man who was sitting there. Moving gracefully, Blair allowed the maître d' to slide the chair under her. As she sat, she noticed that Ronald Herman had dark hair and a beard and mustache. She felt a strange sensation of familiarity.

"Mr. Herman? I'm very pleased to meet you," Blair said as she extended her hand toward him. Blair watched, surprised as Ronald Herman took her hand and, rather than shake it, raised it to his mouth to brush his lips across its back.

"My pleasure," came his somewhat muffled voice.

Blair wished there were more light so she could get a better look at him. But even in the low light she could tell he was handsome.

"Drink?" he asked, his voice a coarse whisper. Then he caughed once, covering his mouth with his hand. "Excuse me, I've a slight cold."

"I'm sorry. A glass of wine would be nice," Blair replied. "And a candle. I can hardly see you," she added.

"Your eyes will adjust," he whispered hoarsely, coughing once again into the back of his hand.

Blair sensed that something was wrong, but she couldn't put her finger on exactly what it was. "I must tell you it's a pleasure to meet you. I'm a fan of yours."

"Really?" he asked in his strangely low voice.

Then, as Ronald Herman had promised, Blair began to get used to the darkness and was able to see him better. His beard was of medium length and almost black, as was his hair. His eyes, beneath bushy brows that did not quite seem to fit the rest of him, were dark—brown or black, she couldn't tell. And although she had never met him, she again felt a tantalizing sense of familiarity about the man.

It was after another moment of silence and of Ronald Herman's intensely scrutinizing gaze that Blair suddenly realized the truth. Her mind grew dark with rage; her breathing deepened with disbelief and anger even as her heart skipped and then began to soar. The world seemed to spin crazily, and she gripped the edge of the table to make it stop.

She felt her blood coursing madly through her body and could hear the labored beating of her pulse. *No,* she screamed silently, but she could not deny the evidence before her.

"How could you?" she demanded in a heated whisper, her eyes misting under the force of this deception.

"Blair—" Sean began, knowing that the charade was over. But she cut him off summarily.

"I don't know what kind of silly game you're playing, but I won't stand for it! Take off that silly disguise, right this minute, or I'll scream my head off!"

"You wouldn't dare," Sean said, grinning boldly at the way she was staring at him.

Amid the confusion in her heart and mind, Blair's eyes narrowed and she pushed her chair back. Taking a deep breath, she never once let her eyes stray from his. Before she could let out the scream she fully intended on issuing, Sean held out his hands in supplication.

Slowly he began to peel the beard from his face. It was tedious work, and not a little painful, but a moment later the false hair was gone.

"The eyebrows," Blair commanded.

Sean sighed and removed the eyebrows, wincing several times as some of his own hair came off with the fake. "Satisfied?" he asked.

"No," she spat, her anger fading although the heartache of seeing him again was still strong. "You're a mean and despicable man."

"No, what I am is a happy man right now," he said, his voice soft, his eyes the same. "Would you have joined me for dinner if I hadn't done this? I don't think so, Blair."

Knowing that he was right, Blair stared at him and willed her once again racing heart to slow, lest she give her emotions away. But no matter how she tried to convince herself of the hopelessness of wanting him and loving him, she realized the inevitability of fate.

Sean, watching the gamut of emotions flickering across her face, saw within them that he had made another mistake. Sadly, he shook his head. "I'm sorry if I disappointed you," he told her, drinking in her beauty yet feeling no guilt for his deception.

Blair shook her head while she tried to sort through her thoughts. "I really would have liked to meet Ronald Herman. I meant it when I told you earlier that I like his novels. It was you at the pool, wasn't it?" she asked suddenly.

Sean nodded. "You mean you don't like my novels?" he asked with a half grin.

Blair smiled suddenly, her anger abating in the face of his boyish grin. "I mean I like Ronald Herman novels. Yours are okay, too," she added teasingly.

Hearing and sensing Blair's changing mood, Sean nodded his head solemnly. "They're one and the same person's work. I didn't deceive you about Ronald Herman. That's the pseudonym I use for my science-fiction novels," Sean admitted.

Blair shook her head again, trying to understand what he was telling her. "Why?"

"It's complicated. Suffice to say, for right now, the two genres I write in don't mix well. Being a success in one could affect the other in ways that I don't want."

Blair, having been involved in the publishing industry for the past four years, thought she understood the reasons for Sean's use of a pseudonym. But that wasn't as important to her as was the reason for his appearance in Mexico City.

"Sean, I..." But whatever she was about to say flew from her mind when he reached across the table and took her hand in his.

"I had to see you again, Blair, I couldn't let things end the way they did at my house."

All the rationalizations she had worked so hard to construct over the past days rose up in her mind. But the barriers of her defenses were being shattered, in this dark and too romantic restaurant, by the warmth of his hand and the crying out of her heart.

She knew she was once again fighting a losing battle and tried to shore up her willpower to defend herself against hurt. But before anything else could happen or be said, the maître d' and the sommelier appeared at the table.

Sean glanced at Blair and saw her face was still stiff with tension. Then he looked at the maître d', who was staring at him in puzzlement, but did not enlighten the man about the disappearance of the beard as he began to order dinner.

While he ordered, he continually glanced at Blair to see if she disagreed with any of his choices. When the maître d' and the wine steward were gone, he smiled at Blair and tightened his hand over hers.

The sensations that filled her left her highly tense but at the same time unafraid. Every movement of his thumb as it massaged the back of her hand sent delicious shivers through her body.

"I think we shocked the maitre d'," Sean said.

A quick laugh escaped her lips. "He couldn't stop looking at you. He had such a funny expression on his face."

"Not quite like yours," Sean told her.

Blair shook her head but did not speak. A moment later the sommelier returned with the white wine and, after presenting the bottle to Sean for his inspection, removed the cork in a theatrical way.

Using a silver tasting spoon that hung from the chain about his neck, he poured a dollop of wine and tasted it. Then he smiled. *"Magnifico!"* he declared. He poured a small amount of the cool white wine into Sean's glass and waited.

Sean obliged him by tasting the wine and nodding his head. The wine steward then filled Blair's crystal goblet and completed filling Sean's. After placing the wine back into the bucket, the sommelier gave them a slight bow and left.

Blair lifted her glass and Sean did the same. "To us," he whispered, touching his glass to hers.

"Is there an us?" Blair asked, her eyes roaming the contours of his face.

"There has to be," he stated.

In that very instant, Blair understood the full extent of her love for Sean. Although she admitted she hadn't known him long enough to feel secure about her emotions, she knew she was deeply, irrevocably, in love with him.

"To us," she said at last as she raised the goblet to her lips.

Sean did not taste the wine as he sipped it; all he could do was gaze at her. Then as he lowered the goblet, he tried to steal a glance at her left hand, but it was curled on the table, and he could not tell if she was wearing her wedding band.

FREE!

It's yours!

THIS BEAUTIFUL AND USEFUL TOTE BAG DESIGNED ESPECIALLY FOR SILHOUETTE...

Return the Silhouette Cameo found on the back, along with your order card today, and you'll also receive the handsome Cameo Tote Bag as an added bonus!

Place this Silhouette token on the order card...

THEN TAKE FOUR <u>FREE</u> BOOKS PLUS A FREE TOTE

Just peel off the Silhouette Cameo and attach it to the postpaid order card. We'll send you 4 FREE novels...a Tote Bag and a chance to preview new books as soon as they are published. See details on your order card.

Don't forget the token!

Silhouette Special Edition ®

120 Brighton Road
P.O. Box 5084
Clifton, NJ 07015-9956

Yes, please send me 4 FREE Silhouette Special Edition novels plus a FREE Tote Bag, without obligation. Unless you hear from me after 1 receive them, send me 6 new Silhouette Special Edition novels to preview for 15 days each month as soon as they are published. I understand that you will bill me just $11.70 for all 6 (a $13.50 value), *with no shipping, handling or other charges of any kind.* There is no minimum number of books that I must buy and I can cancel at any time. The first 4 books and Tote Bag are mine to keep.

NAME _____
(please print)

ADDRESS _____

CITY & STATE _____ ZIP _____

Terms and prices subject to change. Your enrollment is subject to acceptance by Silhouette Books.

SILHOUETTE SPECIAL EDITION is a service mark and registered trademark.

CBS625

Blair, seeing Sean's eyes flicker toward the table, sensed what he was trying to see but did not move her hand.

"Blair," Sean began, but was again interrupted, this time by the waiter who served their appetizer. On each silver serving piece sat three large baked clams swimming in an aromatic sauce.

When the waiter left, he looked at Blair again and smiled tenderly. "We'll talk later, all right?"

The undertone of his words left no doubt in Blair's mind as to what they would be talking about. She nodded in agreement.

They ate the clams slowly, savoring the taste. By the time they finished the appetizer, Blair knew that this night would be like no other in her life.

The entrée arrived, and the waiter refilled their goblets with the dry Spanish wine. The poached salmon was served in a delicate wine sauce and looked as if it should have been framed rather than eaten.

Sean lifted a piece of salmon with his fork and brought it toward his mouth. The fork wavered, and then returned it to the plate. He stared at the woman he had crossed the continent to be with, the woman he could not rid his mind of, and he knew he could wait no longer to speak. He reached for her hand.

Blair's hand met his halfway, and the sudden jolt of electricity from the joining of their fingers took her breath away.

"I love you," Sean said.

"I..." Blair's voice suddenly deserted her, and she had to tell him with her eyes what her voice could not. Sean's other hand stole across the table, palm up, waiting for hers. While her eyes stayed locked with his, she placed her hand in his.

Sean leaned over, even as he raised her hands and kissed her right hand first, his lips gliding over her knuckles slowly. Then he brought her left hand to his mouth and kissed that too, never once letting his eyes wander from hers while he lavished her hands with his mouth's caress.

When Sean released her hands, Blair saw that his breathing was as forced as hers. She noticed, too, that he had studiously avoided looking at her ring finger, nor had his lips touched it when they'd kissed her hand.

Once again, Blair watched Sean lift his fork. This time she smiled when he succeeded in completing the maneuver. Blair tried to eat but could not summon enough strength to lift her fork all the way to her mouth. Finally, she let the fork drop to the plate. "I left it in New York," she told him.

Sean raised his eyebrows.

"My wedding band."

Sean held her open gaze for several seconds before he spoke. "I'm glad. Now eat, it's wonderful."

Blair picked up her fork and began to eat. The admission lifted a heavy weight from her shoulders, and she found as she ate that Sean was right, the food was delicious.

As the rest of the meal passed Blair felt another form of tension settling within her and knew that it was being caused by her knowledge that there could be no turning back now. She could hardly believe that he had told her he loved her, and prayed that he was not deceiving her. She could not bear to lose him again.

By the time coffee was served, two hours had passed and Blair's nerve endings were screaming. She had eaten everything placed in front of her without realizing that she had. After the first bite of salmon, she could no longer taste the food. All she was conscious of was that, with every movement Sean made, a rippling wave of yearning raced through her body. Every gesture he used only served to increase her yearning. Blair had never known this kind of sensual undercurrent before and was hard pressed to fully understand it.

Blair sighed in relief when the captain finally brought the check for Sean to sign, and at long last they stood and left the dining room.

"I'm stuffed," Sean admitted unromantically. "Shall we take a walk?"

"Please," Blair replied, needing more time to think and to understand this strong physical need that was close to overwhelming her.

Sean guided them through the lobby and out onto the street. Although it was Sunday night, the street was busy. They walked hand in hand for several blocks, gazing into the windows of the shops that lined the boulevard. A half hour later, they returned to the hotel.

Once inside the lobby, tension again captured Blair, but she was able to relax when Sean continued past the bank of elevators and led her into the lounge. There they sat at a small table near the dance floor and ordered drinks. Blair asked for a Lillet, Sean a cognac.

The band that was now playing was different from the one Blair had heard when she'd first gone to the dining room. This quartet was playing romantic songs that cried out to be danced to.

Standing without speaking, Sean took Blair's hand and helped her to rise. They walked to the highly polished dance floor, and still without speaking, Sean slipped his arm around her back and drew her close.

Blair leaned upon the hardness of Sean's chest, letting the gentle heat of his body soothe her tortured nerves as she and Sean danced slowly to the music. His warm breath whispered across her cheek. She closed her eyes and rested her head on his shoulder. Their thighs were touching, and heat began to build within her. She could feel every inch of his body against hers, and she bathed within the envelope of love and desire that contained them.

"I've missed you," Sean said as he inhaled the fragrance from her hair.

Blair lifted her head to gaze into his eyes. She saw the truth of his words written there and knew she must speak now or she would never be able to say what must be said.

"Sean," she began, brushing her lips across his before she went on. She had been wanting to do that all night—just taste his lips once. "I'm still the same person I was in Pennsylvania. I still believe in the same values. It can't be a casual affair, it must be all or nothing."

Then Blair waited, her breath held while she stood beneath his scrutiny. Finally, a shadowy smile softened his mouth.

"I don't tell a casual affair that I love her." Sean lowered his head and kissed her deeply, tasting the well-remembered sweet warmth of her mouth.

Blair was paralyzed, unable to move as his lips covered hers. She felt the kiss with her whole being, felt it from her mouth to her toes, and by the time he released her, she could not move to the music any longer.

Slowly, as one song ended and another began, Sean continued to guide her on the dance floor, his lips always touching some part of her—her ears, her neck, her mouth.

After an eternity of music and movement, they returned to their table and slowly, as if time held no meaning, finished their drinks. Neither talked, they just gazed deeply and lovingly at each other until Sean stood and offered her his hand.

"It's time," he said.

A chill of anticipation raced through her when she stood. Blair's hand tightened on his as she smiled softly. "Yes, I think our time has come," she replied.

And please, she prayed, *let him stay this time, let him stay forever.*

Chapter Eight

For the second time that day, Blair had no memory of the elevator ride. There was only the awareness that she was taking the next step forward with her life. Leaning against Sean in the elevator, Blair was bathed in the powerful aura surrounding him. His eyes—deep, burning circles gazing into the very depths of her soul—held hers for thirty-two stories. His arm was around her. His fingers, constantly moving on her back, sent a raging river of current through her body. His warm breath on her cheek reminded Blair of a tropical breeze that caressed her skin with gentleness.

They walked from the elevator to the door in the same envelope of silence that had engulfed them since they'd left the lounge. Their very silence was more comforting to Blair than any words of reassurance could have been.

"Key," Sean whispered in her ear.

"Mmmm," she replied absently as she reached into her clutch and fumbled through it. When she found the key, she withdrew it and handed it to Sean. The instant their fingers touched, the electricity began to flow again.

After Sean opened the door, Blair, feeling suddenly shy, entered the room. She captured her lower lip between her teeth as her old doubts surfaced. *Am I sure,* she asked herself. But it was Sean's lips on the back of her neck that gave her the answer. *Yes.*

Walking slowly, Blair reached for the small lamp on the dresser. When she turned it on, the room was bathed in its soft light. She gazed at Sean but was still afraid to speak, afraid to trust her voice not to break the magic of this night.

"Come outside with me," Sean commanded as he strode past her and opened the balcony door. Blair watched the door open and Sean disappear into the night.

As she went toward the balcony, she heard a popping sound, and once she was outside, she saw Sean pouring champagne into two tulip glasses.

"I hope you don't mind that I took the liberty of ordering a celebration for us?" he asked, smiling disarmingly at the same time.

"You were very confident," Blair said, and even as she spoke she wanted to take back the sharpness of her words.

Sean did not let his smile fade; rather, he waited for a moment before he replied. When he did, his words were as serious as his voice.

"Without my confidence, I wouldn't be here, pouring this champagne, would I? Blair, my confidence is more important to me than money."

"Are you that rich?" she asked, her words and manner emphasizing the levity she was trying to achieve.

"In many things," he replied gravely.

Despite the seriousness of his reply, Blair saw his eyes were sparkling with humor. "Sean," Blair whispered a moment later, hating herself for what her mind was commanding her to voice but unwilling to let it stay within her.

Before she could continue, Sean handed her a champagne-filled glass. A moment later, high above Mexico City, the sound of their glasses touching rang beautifully in the night air. She took a sip of the dry, sparkling liquid and felt another shiver run the length of her body. It had not been induced by the champagne but by the way Sean was looking at her.

"Yes?" Sean asked, reminding Blair that she had started to speak to him. He knew almost intuitively what she was going to say, and knew too that those words needn't be said aloud.

"I...we have to talk, just as we said at dinner. Stop looking at me like that!" she ordered, unable to stand against the force of his eyes. Turning, she looked away from him for a moment and took another sip of champagne, which, she realized belatedly, was the best she'd ever tasted.

Blair felt him come up behind her and sighed when his hand slipped around her waist. Involuntarily she leaned back upon his tall and muscular frame. Taking another deep breath, Blair rebuilt her determination and began to speak again, knowing that what she was about to say could either ruin the magic of the most special of nights or make it even better.

"I'm not like the women you know," she said as she watched the glittering lights that spread out below her. "I need more than empty words and a famous man. I need love, and I need to share that love, not just give it or receive it. I need the commitment and sharing of my life with the man I love, and I will not settle for less than I once had. And, Sean," she said, turning to face him, "I will not be used."

Silence reigned supreme while Blair held her breath and her nerves grew explosively taut under the pressure of waiting to learn her fate. She was overly aware that even when she'd turned, his arm had not moved away, and his hand had resettled into the small of her back.

Leaning down, Sean brushed his lips along her cheek, tightened his arm around her and drew her closer. When he spoke, his voice was low and husky, and he stared deeply into her eyes. "I don't love frivolously. Nor could I love a woman who wants me because of my name. Blair, I want you as I've never wanted another woman. It seems I've been waiting an eternity for you. I can't wait any longer. You have my love, you always have."

Blair's head swam amid his words as her breath once again returned to her body. He had said everything she had wanted, everything she had needed from that first moment her hip had brushed against his in Pennsylvania.

She waited as he lowered his mouth to hers. The champagne that spilled from her glass onto her hand went unnoticed as they kissed. For a long time, they remained with their bodies pressed closely together. Their lips hungrily devoured each other's and their tongues wove together in love and passion.

But finally Sean drew away. Taking the champagne glass from her, he placed it and his on the small table. Then he reached out his hand for Blair and waited.

When the heated softness of her hand was in his, he lifted it to his lips. Smiling, he saw the film of champagne coating her skin. "Dom Perignon is for the lips and stomach, not the hand," he told her as he drew the moisture from her skin with his mouth.

Blair felt as though she were inside a tornado, her hand aflame, her mind spinning in a whirlwind of desire and need, until Sean slowly lowered her hand and drew her into the room. When the door was closed behind them, Blair turned to him. "Sean," she whispered.

"No more words," he said as his mouth covered hers and he kissed her deeply.

Blair's body turned to molten fire as every inch of his body pressed upon hers. The warm, wonderful sensation of her breasts pushing against his chest was overwhelming. When his mouth left hers and a moment later branded the skin on her neck, her hands rose to weave through his soft jet hair, and pressed his lips harder to her skin.

His hands loosened their grip on her back and began to explore her curves. Slowly one hand cupped her rear, bringing her tighter to him. The other hand ran in circles on her back, gently and teasingly sending shivers of anticipation to every part of her.

Sean drew back. His eyes devoured her face hungrily. "I must love you now," he said, his voice turning raspy with his need.

Blair nodded slowly, unable even to whisper the words that echoed his so exactly.

She went to him again, and he half lifted, half carried her to the bed. Blair floated only inches above the floor, held securely by the strength of the man she loved. Before she realized it, the bed was beneath her and the weight of Sean above. His hands and mouth were everywhere, his lips scorching the skin they touched as his hands explored her body through the thin material of the dress.

Blair's own hands moved without command, going to his jacket and sliding it from his shoulders. As she did that, Sean sat up. Only then did Blair open her eyes to see him smiling down at her. Blair could not help but return the smile.

"You are beautiful," he stated while he stood and removed his jacket. Then she watched, her heart beating faster and faster, as he took off his shirt. His chest was broad, and a dark mat of curly hair covered the sleekness of his muscles. When he began to undo his trousers, Blair grew shy.

"The light," she whispered.

"I want to see you."

"Please, Sean, turn off the light." Sean paused to gaze at her. He walked to the dresser, and dimmed the lamp. A heartbeat later, moonlight filtered through the glass door of the balcony, illuminating the room as no artificial light could.

Blair heard the whisper of material dropping to the floor before Sean returned to her side again. But as she sat up, he stopped her. Slowly his hands went to the back of her dress, and while his fingers searched for the zipper, his lips touched the sensitive skin at the joining of her neck and shoulder. Blair inhaled sharply at the heated contact, her entire body tensing with her powerful reaction. And as the heat of his lingering kiss dissipated along her shoulder, she heard the sound of her zipper being released.

When Sean slipped the dress from her shoulders, he pulled her to her feet and the dress fell to her ankles. But Sean's eyes were locked upon hers, and refused to look elsewhere. When he finally moved again, it was only his hands that did. His eyes stayed fixed upon hers while his fingers sought the catch of her bra. An instant later the material parted, and her breasts came free.

And still Sean's eyes did not leave hers. He slid the bra from her shoulders and let it fall from his fingers. Then he moved. He came against her, and for the first time her bare breasts touched his skin. She finally felt the unmasked heat and firmness of his skin on hers while his mouth devoured hers and his tongue probed within the welcoming warmth of her mouth.

His desire was hard against her skin, and she knew his need matched hers. When he suddenly moved his lips to travel downward, she cried out in anguish. Then his mouth was on her breast, and her legs were trembling madly. His lips burned the surface of her breasts even as her hands grasped his head and held it to her.

His hands slid into the waistband of her panties, and she shivered at the tingling sensation of the silk in its pathway down her legs. Sean knelt and lifted one of her feet. Panty and shoe came away together. He re-

peated the process again, until at last Blair was as na-
ked as he. Ever so slowly Sean rose up along her body,
until he lifted her once again from the floor and set her
gently upon the bed.

Blair's eyes misted as she gazed at the man standing above her. Her body was out of control, and her
yearning was close to pain. But even so her mind was
crystal clear, and she knew exactly what she was doing
and why. She watched, her breasts rising and falling in
the pale moonlight, as he lowered himself to her. His
mouth went to her left breast and lances of fire shot
inward.

Sean drew in her stiffened nipple to taste its velvet
softness. His hands roamed along her length, skim-
ming along her silken skin, exploring and learning
everything that he could about the beautiful woman
he was with.

His mouth followed his hands, traveling everywhere they did and caressing Blair's vibrantly alive
skin. His fingers dipped to touch the tender insides of
her thighs even as his mouth rose up again to lavish her
other breast with heated kisses before taking its hardened peak within his lips.

He heard Blair's labored breathing and the low cries
of pleasure that came from her and soon he could not
hold himself back any longer. Lifting up, he gazed
unabashadly at her, taking the time to savor the beauty
of her alabaster skin and the perfection of her body.

When Sean's mouth left her breast that final time,
and he rose up above her, Blair's eyes widened, and
she read the love on his face. Her breath caught when
he moved to fit himself upon her. His eyes, so dark, so
passionate, called to her, and Blair lifted her head and

drank of his male beauty as he pulled her to him and entered her slowly.

Blair cried out at his gentle yet burning entrance. And then all movement stopped. Her breasts were crushed to his chest; her nipples tingled with the sensation of his hair upon them.

Her legs wound around his hips, and her arms locked onto his back. Heat raced through her body, and a volcano of need and desire exploded deep within her very core.

Sean held himself under tight control after he delved so deeply within Blair. When her legs and arms secured him to her, his mind and body became awash in the incredible woman he had joined with. Her silken skin sent waves of heat racing through him, building his needs to even greater heights.

He drew his mouth from hers and gazed at her face. Slowly, even as his eyes returned to hers, he moved again within her feminine warmth.

Blair responded totally to Sean, matching him eagerly in her own quest to give her love. Reality departed from this soft cloud they shared high above the world. All thought left her while Sean carried her away to a different place, a place where she'd never been before. Every sense was alive, every part of her body became a part of his. They had become one, she knew, and it was something that had never happened before.

Blair was his, as she knew he was hers. Higher and higher Blair soared, her mind apart from her body yet completely alive and sharing in every moment of their lovemaking. Then her body exploded. She felt the fire start deep within her, and expand to every part of her.

Her body acted without guidance as it arched to meet his, even as she felt Sean burst forth within her.

Ever so slowly, Blair's breathing began to gentle. But when Sean started to lift himself from her, she held him fast.

He kissed her lovingly. "I'm too heavy for you," he whispered.

"You'll never be too heavy," she said, her eyes flickering across her face. "You fit," she stated with finality.

They stayed together for a long time, holding each other as their hands wandered in soft caressing motions. When Sean finally moved, he slipped gently from her to lie on his back. At the same time, he drew Blair into the crook of his arm. She rested her head on his shoulder and lightly draped one arm across his chest.

"I've never felt anything like that before," she hesitantly admitted. Sean pulled her closer to him as his lips forced their way through her curls to kiss the crown of her head.

"It had to be that way, my love, it had to be," he said. They were silent for a long time after that, and slowly, without wanting it to happen, Blair felt sleep overtaking her. As the veil of dreams descended, she heard Sean whisper good-night.

It was sometime before dawn that Blair awoke. Fire burned across her abdomen; hands caressed her breasts. As she came slowly to awareness, Sean's mouth was on hers. Seconds later Blair was lost in their lovemaking and was transported aloft, once again to find herself floating on a cloud of desire and joy. When their lovemaking ended, they lay side by side, holding each other close. Again Blair began to drift into sleep, but before she would allow herself to become oblivious she moved her mouth to Sean's ear.

"I love you." She finally said aloud to him what her eyes and body and every gesture had already told him. She heard Sean's gentle sigh as he pulled her closer to him.

Sunlight streamed in through the glass door, calling Blair to meet the day. Stretching luxuriously, she opened her eyes. The memory of the past night filtered into her mind, and she quickly turned her head. Sean was gone!

Blair bit her lip at the harsh realization of just how much she had let herself go. *And now he's gone. What have I done?* Blair stared at the pillow that still held the indentation of Sean's head, and slowly traced its depth with a tentative finger. She could smell his scent in the bed, and a wave of sadness washed over her. *Why had he left?*

She had believed him last night, totally believed everything he'd said. *Am I that gullible?*

"Good morning," came Sean's deep voice, shattering the quiet of the room.

Turning quickly, Blair saw him wheeling a food cart through the connecting door.

"Yes, I live next door. The boy next door and all..." he teased with a smile. But when he saw the look on her face, his smile fled. Leaving the cart where it was, he went to her. "Regrets?" he asked tenderly as he stroked her cheek with his fingers.

"Teeth," Blair replied, trying to avoid voicing what she had felt seconds before.

"Teeth?" he asked, puzzled.

"Brush my teeth," Blair told him, barely opening her lips.

"Ah...the wine, champagne and Mexican food. Dragon's breath!" he declared with a smile. Without allowing her to escape, he drew her to him and kissed her. When he released her, he smiled and declared, "Dragon's breath and all, I'll take you!"

Blair felt the warm rush of blood flowing beneath the surface of her skin and knew Sean could see the redness covering her from navel to forehead. Without saying another word, she rolled to the other side of the bed, slipped to the carpet and ran into the bathroom. Behind her Sean's laughter echoed brightly.

As she was brushing her teeth, Sean knocked on the bathroom door. "Uhmmm?"

"Don't take too long, love, breakfast is awaiting you."

Blair smiled and turned on the shower. She showered quickly, but at the same time was reluctant to wash all of the past night away. Then, with a feeling of growing confidence, she knew that there would be many more nights of love in their future. "An eternity," Sean had said.

Breakfast on the sun-drenched balcony was wonderful. The warmth of the morning sun on her as she drank the strong Mexican coffee and ate hot biscuits dripping with melted butter made Blair even more aware of the change in her life. She was more alive, more responsive to everything, than she'd been in years. And she knew with full acceptance that the past had been put to rest and the future stretched invitingly ahead of her.

"I love the way you smile," Sean said after watching her for several moments.

"Is that what attracted you...my smile?" she asked, looking at him over the rim of her cup.

"You never smiled the night of the party, not once."

"But you did," she replied.

"That's part of my persona. I have to smile or be stoic on cue. The public demands it," he informed her in half serious tones.

"Yes. And I'm sure the blonde demanded indifference." Blair looked quickly away the moment she finished, surprised at herself for daring to say what she had. But Sean's thunderous laugh startled her and made her look back at him.

"Do I detect a streak of jealousy? You didn't even know me or like me then," he told her, grinning boldly.

"You're right, I didn't know you then. Why would I be jealous?" she asked, but the knowledge that he had seen through her piqued her pride.

"And you don't want to know who she was either, do you?"

"Why should I?" Blair challenged, arching her eyebrows. "As long as *she's* in the past."

Again Sean laughed, and felt a swelling of emotion for her, while he silently applauded the way she was handling his teasing.

"Do you know that if another man had walked up to you that night, I would have..."

"Stop!" Blair ordered, laughing at the animation in his face. "You hadn't even spoken to me then. Besides, you had your *blonde*," she reminded him pointedly.

"The minute you walked into the room there was no one else there, only you," Sean stated, his voice deepening into a husky drawl.

Blair saw within the depths of his eyes that every word he said was the truth. "And I suppose you didn't take the blonde home either?"

Sean didn't smile. "I don't mix business with pleasure.... At least not until I met you."

"Business? She was business?" Blair asked, confused.

"Her name is Joyce Leonard, and she is—"

"Your editor," Blair said, recognizing the woman's name immediately. "Oh...Sean...I think I just embarrassed myself—again."

"You never have to feel embarrassed with me. Besides," he said, grinning at the sweet expression on her face, "I like learning that you were jealous then."

"I wasn't jealous," she retorted.

Sean didn't say anything; instead, he put his cup down and stood. He went over to her, took the coffee cup out of her hands and slowly drew her to her feet.

Blair watched in silent fascination when his mouth crushed down upon hers. But she could not keep her eyes open as the memory of the previous night flooded into her head. Her body filled with a sudden desire that left her weak and clutching him for support. Taking a deep shuddering breath when the kiss had ended, Blair pushed Sean away.

"Don't kiss me like that! I have work to do today," she told him in a shaky voice.

"Take the day off," he countered as he took in the heavy rise and fall of her breasts.

"No, Sean. There's a very real deadline," she reminded him with a smile of regret. Lifting her hand, she traced the outline of his mouth with her fingertips.

"Later," Sean promised, capturing her hand and kissing each fingertip in turn. Then he released her hand and returned to the table, lifting the coffee carafe as he did. "One more cup to start the day?"

"One more," she agreed.

"Where are you going today?"

"First to the hall of records to see if I can locate anything at all about Marylena Montez. If I can, I'll trace the information from there. Then I'll try the historical societies, and as a last resort the libraries."

"Why as a last resort?" Sean asked, puzzled by her statement.

"Only if Marylena was a very famous person, which we already know she wasn't, would I go to the library first. Where would I find information on her in the library? I doubt if there's been a biography written about her."

Sean nodded. "Your point's well taken. That's why you're the researcher, not me."

"Exactly."

"But don't be too disappointed by the record-keeping system. Marylena Montez lived here over two hundred years ago, and there may be very little evidence left of her," Sean warned.

"If there's anything to find," Blair declared as she took another sip of coffee, "I'll find it."

Sean nodded when he saw the intensity of her words reflected in her eyes. "I know you will, Blair, I know you will."

"What will you do today?" Blair asked.

"What I do best. I have my typewriter with me to wile away the hours until you return."

Blair made a mew at his half-jesting words, but the sparkle in his eyes told her that, as light as the words were, he meant them.

"I love you," she whispered.

Chapter Nine

The hall of records smelled like the mausoleum it was. The records of Mexican history predated those of the United States. Thankful for her fluency in Spanish, Blair was able to get everything she needed with the least amount of wasted time. However, she knew it had been her purposely sultry voice and flirtatious manner that had helped to get her the information from the clerks. But without her ability to speak Spanish, all the flirting in the world would not have helped.

Taking everything she'd gotten with her, Blair went to the small desk one of the clerks had made available to her. As she sat and looked at the records, a sigh escaped her lips. No matter how hard she tried, she could not stop Sean's face from floating before her.

"Leave me alone," she whispered.

"Pardon, senorita?" asked the secretary at the next desk.

"Es nada. Gracias," she told the woman as she felt a blush rise on her cheeks. *I have to stop that too,* she chided herself. Blair thought she'd blushed more since meeting Sean than she had in her entire life.

Once again she bent to study the records. Slowly, as the story began to unfold, Blair became immersed within the life of the Montezes, and especially Marylena Montez.

Blair learned from piecing the different record entries together that Marylena Montez had actually lived and that she had been the daughter of Don Vasco De Legro De Montez, a direct descendant of Spanish royalty. The Montez family had crossed the ocean in the seventeenth century and, after arriving in Mexico, had become one of the largest and wealthiest landowners in the country. Their lands stretched along the coast deep into California, which at the time belonged to Mexico and Spain.

And as she expected, most of what she learned from the old records dealt with the Montez men and their legal dealings. Only the births of Marylena, her two sisters and three brothers told of the actual family. All the other record notices were about the lands they owned and the governmental and military dealings that Don Vasco and his heirs had been involved with.

The one other thing that Blair discovered, after another hour of searching through the musty pages, was that there was no death notice posted for Marylena Montez as there were notices for her siblings.

Finally, Blair returned the documents to the respective clerks, and left the government building before heading toward her next stop.

A small and private historical foundation was Blair's next destination. Once there, she spoke with the woman in charge. Senora Herrara was a stately, handsome woman of sixty, whose long gray hair was done up in a tight bun and covered with the delicate web of a silken hair net. Her dress was conservatively modern; her voice was authoritative.

Blair liked her immediately and soon broke through the woman's initial reserve. Because of the nature of Sean's book, Blair had originally determined that to tell the truth about her research would gain her disdain at best. She explained to Senora Herrera that she was researching the life of Marylena Montez for a section of a book that would deal with the Spanish aristocracy and love.

Blair sensed she had been right in her decision when she saw the historian's eyes glow. Soon Blair had several volumes of Mexican history dealing with the Montez family, dating from the time of Don Vasco's landing in the New World, and she was overjoyed by her luck.

Blair read for two straight hours, fascinated by the rich history and tradition of the Montez family. By one o'clock she had learned much about the first twelve years of Marylena Montez's life. She was so absorbed with her research that she did not hear Senora Herrera's polite cough. But at the second, more insistent cough, Blair looked up.

"I'm sorry, senorita, but it is time to close for lunch and siesta," the older woman informed Blair in Spanish.

Blair was stricken, and was sure that her face reflected the fact that she did not want to wait another two hours to finish with her research, But she also knew that she should not argue or impose on the woman.

With a knowing smile on her lips, the older woman spoke again. This time it was not in Spanish, but in lightly accented English. "I see how important this is to you, and I am sorry, but the rule is that we must close." Senora Herrara paused for a moment as if in debate with herself.

"Perhaps you would care to join me for lunch? I can practice my English and tell you a little more about our history?"

"Thank you," Blair said, immediately accepting the offer.

"Come then," Senora Herrera said. "You can leave the books there until you return."

Blair rose and followed as the stately woman locked the front door and then led her to the back of the building. It was only then that Blair realized the small building was more than just an historical society. It was also Senora Herrara's home.

Blair followed the woman through two more large rooms and then out another door and into a patio surrounded by brick walls lined with tall hedges. A cool breeze floated tantalizingly through the air and, while Blair looked around, a young, dark-skinned girl appeared. Blair thought her to be part Indian.

Senora Herrera spoke to the girl in Spanish. The girl left a moment later, only to return with a silver tray that held two bowls of salad, two crystal wineglasses, and a carafe of light red wine.

After the servant had placed the food on the table, Senora Herrera motioned for Blair to sit as the serving girl poured the wine.

The older woman smiled encouragingly at Blair and began to eat. Blair ate, too, pleasantly surprised at the cool, crisp taste of the fresh salad. A few minutes later Blair took a sip of the wine.

"Delicious," she said, breaking the comfortable silence.

"I'm glad you like it. It comes from my family's vineyards."

"Really?" Blair asked in surprise.

Senora Herrera nodded proudly. "My family has been in Mexico for a long, long time," she said with a smile that fully showed her pride.

"Your English is perfect," Blair stated. "You didn't need me to practice with. But I'll hold you to your promise of the history," she said in a friendly manner.

"And I thought it was only the American men who were so impatient. Women must have patience, no?" she asked, smiling as she did. Then the older woman's face turned serious. "Unless of course love has taken you and you are anxious to return to his arms...."

Blair was again unable to control her blush.

"Ah, yes!" Senora Herrera declared.

"The Montez family? Are you familiar with them? Especially anything about Marylena Montez?" Blair asked in an effort to change the subject her benefactor had begun.

"Very familiar," Senora Herrera stated with a smile of remembrance on her face. "You see, my husband's family is Herrera; however, my maiden name is Marylena Consuela de Montez."

Blair's fork froze halfway to her mouth. Her senses were assaulted by a combination of disbelief, fright, and on the heels of those, excitement. She was undeniably glad to find an actual descendant of the woman she was researching, but finding a woman with the same name scared her too.

"Marylena..." Blair whispered, shaking her head.

Senora Marylena Herrera nodded solemnly. "Shall I tell you about the woman I was named for?"

Blair, speechless, could only nod in answer and take another sip of wine, still unable to believe this was really happening.

"Good, because that is why you are here. As you have already learned from the material I gave you, the Montez family was wealthy—perhaps the wealthiest of all Spanish nobility in the Americas. Their lands stretched from Santa Barbara to Mazatlán. They owned huge herds of cattle and produced the best grapes for the finest wines. They were a proud family, and Don Vasco was the proudest of men.

"The Montez family flourished in their new home, ruling it as they had their lands in Spain. They were honest, fair, and above all, chivalrous." The older woman paused for a moment to gaze into Blair's hazel eyes, and saw the power her words had over her guest.

"Let me explain about the strange combination of Marylena's name. She was so named because of an ancestor—the sister of the Queen of Spain—who had borne twin girls. She had already decided upon the name Marie Elaina if she had a daughter. She would not change her mind when there were twins. Instead, she condensed the name and named the first born Marylena and the second born Marie Elaina. In our family, the tradition grew to always name the first born Marylena and the next Marie Elaina.

"Marylena Montez was the youngest child of Don Vasco's family, and her story has been handed down through each generation. It is a very sad story," Senora Herrera told Blair. "She was the favorite of Don Vasco and the image of her mother. Emeralda Carenna, Marylena's mother, was so beautiful a woman that her suitors had begun to court her when she was only eleven. Her father, a Castilian duke, would have none of the men and protected her until she was fifteen.

"It was shortly after Emeralda turned sixteen that Don Vasco saw her for the first time. She was tall for a Spanish woman, with flashing blue eyes and dark, shining hair. Don Vasco won her heart from her and her hand in marriage from her father.

"Marylena, from the age of three, was the exact image of her mother, and Don Vasco treated her as a princess. Everything was wonderful then. The family was close and they all loved and respected each other." Senora Herrera stopped talking to take a sip of wine and to study Blair.

To Blair, it was as if she were back in school and the woman sitting near her, her teacher. She waited silently but knew her eyes showed her unabashed pleading for more.

When the older woman continued, her tone changed. "As custom decreed for all noble Spanish families in Mexico, the boys, when they turned nine, were sent back to Spain to be educated properly. The girls were taught by priests, and each learned to read and write Spanish and Latin. They were taught history and religion along with those things that every woman of royalty must know. But when Marylena turned fourteen, her life changed.

"At fourteen, she fell in love. Ah, you say, love is wonderful," Senora Herrera said to Blair with a knowing smile. Then she shook her head sadly. "But not for a girl in Marylena's position. For her, love should have been chosen carefully—she was to love only someone of the correct station. Sadly, Marylena fell in love with the boy who cared for the horses.

"They say he was a handsome lad, with dark Spanish eyes and hair the color of midnight."

"Black?" Blair asked, feeling a shiver as she thought of Sean's beautiful jet hair and deep brown eyes.

"As black as midnight," the older woman said with a nod. "But he was baseborn, and it was wrong. They loved each other deeply and silently, both knowing that they could not speak of their love or acknowledge it at all. But a glance was all that was necessary for them to show their true feelings.

"Three years passed and soon Marylena's parents became worried. All the men who had paid court to their daughter had been rejected by her. The most handsome of men, the richest and most noble, were all turned away by Marylena.

"One night Marylena's mother came to her. She told her that Marylena must choose a husband, for she was almost past the proper age for marriage. Because of the importance of the family, she must marry.

"Marylena protested, crying and begging, but it was all to no avail. Then, because of the love she had always had for her mother, she confessed the true reason why she could not choose a husband. She told of her love for the stable boy, Raul. Her mother was shocked beyond reason, unable to understand how such a thing could have happened. She left her daughter and went to Don Vasco to tell him the story.

"The very next day, Don Vasco had to do the one thing that he had never thought he would have to. He summoned Marylena and, after hearing the shaming story from her own lips, told her that he had no choice but to decide on a husband for her and see her married within the month.

"Marylena ran from her father, knowing that life for her had ended. Somehow she had always hoped she would be able to overcome her father's objections and marry her true love.

"Later that morning, Marylena was able to sneak out of the house. When she did, she went to where she knew Raul would be. Finding him, she told Raul everything that had happened, and begged him to run away with her. But Raul, loving her as deeply as he did, would not run away with her; he would not bring her into the unhappy and harsh life of a peasant.

"Marylena cried, and for the first time since he'd set eyes on Marylena, Raul gathered her within his arms and kissed her. It was during the first kiss that the lovers had shared that Don Vasco came upon them. So enraged was he that he took the boy and began to beat him.

"Marylena attacked her father, trying to protect her love. She begged her father to spare Raul. But only when she threatened to commit the most mortal of sins—suicide—did Don Vasco's sanity return.

"Don Vasco then had young Raul taken from his lands with the order that if he ever returned to shame Don Vasco and his family, his life would be forfeit. With a last look at the woman he loved, Raul was taken from Montez lands. Four weeks later, Marylena was married to her third cousin Edwardo De-Silva and taken to the DeSilva lands in Monterey."

Blair was thoroughly shaken when Marylena finished her story. Although she had known to a small degree from listening to Dr. Eldridge's tapes of the present-day man who claimed to be the reincarnation of Marylena Montez's doomed lover, Raul, Senora Herrera's story had touched her so deeply that tears spilled from her eyes without her realizing it.

Before Blair could say anything, the young servant girl came over to the table and cleared away the dishes. Then she placed two bone-china teacups and saucers before the women. Blair was mesmerized by the intricate white floral design on each cup. The servant poured the tea and disappeared from the patio.

"These cups are heirlooms of the Montez family," Senora Herrera told her.

"What happened to Marylena after she married DeSilva?" Blair asked, swallowing hard to ease the emotions that still filled her mind.

"She gave birth to a son, Fernando DeSilva. Then Marylena, having done her duty as a wife, entered a convent, never again to return to the outside world."

Blair watched as Senora Herrera's eyes filmed with moisture, and felt her own doing the same again.

"In the convent she assumed the name Elaina. She became Sister Elaina when Edwardo DeSilva died, and she was widowed and allowed to become a nun."

"She never saw Raul again?" Blair asked in a husky voice.

"To no one's knowledge. The last time she had seen her true love had been that morning when her father had banished him and doomed her."

"Thank you," Blair whispered, trying ineffectually to chase away the lump that filled her throat.

"You are most welcome. I find myself glad to have shared some of my own history with you," Senora Herrera told Blair in a grave voice.

Once again Blair stood on the high balcony, her arms crossed and her hands on her shoulders as she looked down upon the twinkling vista of Mexico City. The warm air caressed her skin and dipped into the opening of the negligee she wore, causing her skin to grow taut.

Dropping her arms, she ran her hands down her sides. The feel of the satin nightgown brought the memory of the gift back into her thoughts.

She and Sean had dined in the hotel restaurant again, and afterward they'd spent a few hours dancing in the lounge. Throughout dinner and the time they'd danced, Blair had retold the story of Marylena

Montez, emphasizing the factuality of Dr. Eldridge's patient's past-life memories.

While Sean had listened intently to her, he had nodded occasionally. But at one point in her story, he had smiled with some secret knowledge that had disturbed her for a moment.

When she had finished her tale, Sean told her that she'd done a wonderful job and that he would make reservations for their return to New York.

Yet throughout the evening and well into the night, a strange lethargy had held Blair's mind captive. She could not rid her thoughts of the story, not even when she danced close to Sean. Finally, Sean's loving kisses had lifted up her spirits. But even so, to a small degree, the sadness of Marylena Montez's life hundreds of years before haunted her.

When they had returned to her room and were at the door, she'd glanced at Sean and sensed a mysterious air surrounding him. Upon entering, he'd pointed toward the bed and the gift-wrapped box lying upon it. He'd told her it was a gift, not just for her, but for both of them. "I understand your modesty," he'd told her, "and I love you for it."

When she had started to open it, Sean had gone through the connecting door and into his room to change out of his evening clothes.

When she'd stripped the golden paper from the box and opened it, her breath had escaped with a gasp. Slowly she'd lifted a satin nightgown out of the box and stared at its shimmering beauty in surprise.

Her first reaction had been one of shock. Then she'd gotten angry at his assumption. And then she'd realized he was right. She was modest, and she had felt self-conscious about walking around the room without her clothes on. And she had not brought anything to lounge in except for a few T-shirts to wear to bed. She hadn't expected to be seeing anyone at night.

A moment later Blair had gone into the bathroom and changed out of the dress she had worn and into the soft negligee. When she'd studied herself in the mirror, she had sighed with approval.

The fit was perfect and the gown clung to her curves seductively while hiding what she considered her weaker spots.

The solid material of the bodice exposed only the very tops of her high breasts. The bodice was laced up the center and did not meet until the material closed just above her navel. Yet as immodest as it had looked, the seven satin buttons, which fitted into seven satin loops, had been sufficient to turn the negligee into a less revealing gown that had made Blair feel soft, feminine and comfortable.

After leaving the bathroom and discovering that Sean had not yet returned, Blair had gone out onto the balcony to await him.

She didn't hear Sean come up behind her, and only realized he was there when his hand touched her shoulder and drew her from her thoughts. Back in the present, Blair smiled as she covered his hand with hers and leaned back against him.

"I love you," he whispered. "And I'm glad you weren't offended by the gift."

"Thank you," Blair replied as she closed her eyes dreamily. "I was angry for a moment...but only a moment. It's beautiful."

"As you are," Sean told her, bending his head to breathe in the scent rising from her hair. He had been worried that she would misinterpret the reason for the negligee, and was glad she hadn't. "Besides, I like giving you pretty things," he added just before his lips touched her cheek.

Blair felt the familiar heat of her desire for him grow the moment his lips touched her skin. "We'll be in New York soon. I'm going to miss it here."

"I'll bring you back, I promise," Sean told her. "And we won't be going back to New York tomorrow."

Blair's eyes snapped open as she turned to face him, dislodging his hands as she whirled. "What do you mean? I thought you were going to make the reservations?"

"I just did. We're leaving the day after tomorrow," he informed her with his usual confident smile.

"Sean," she began patiently, "we've only a little over two weeks left to complete the research. I have to get back to New York," she stated, doing her best to ignore his boyish grin.

"But not tomorrow. Tomorrow is a day off, a busman's holiday so to speak." Sean paused, his eyes roaming across her face, drinking in the beauty they continually discovered. "And it's a day to celebrate."

"Celebrate what?" she asked, unable to keep the tension from her voice at this new development.

"This," Sean said as he slipped his hand into the pocket of his robe. When he withdrew it, there was a small midnight-blue velvet box in his hand.

Blair stared at it, and then at him. Her breathing had suddenly stopped.

"I think you should take it now," Sean coaxed gently.

Blair's fingers shook as she lifted the box from his palm. Holding it in her left hand, she slowly opened it. For the second time that night, she gasped. Staring up at her was a large, square-cut emerald, its green fires glowing daringly. Her heart pounded wildly as her eyes returned to Sean's.

"It's...it's magnificent."

"No, it's your engagement ring," he replied in a husky voice. "Will you marry me?"

"I..." But Blair could not speak. All she could do was look at Sean and try to control the wild racing of her heart.

"Here," Sean offered, "let me help you." Taking the velvet box from her hand, he put it in his own. After he took the ring out, he turned her left hand over and slowly slipped the ring onto her finger.

Blair stared at her hand the whole while until the green flames of the emerald dissolved into a myriad of wet sparkles.

"Tears, too? But you haven't answered me yet," he said, drawing her close to him and tilting her head toward his at the same time.

"But I have," Blair said as she raised up to meet his lips. The saltiness of her tears mingled with the kiss, but Blair did not taste them. She would be his wife, and that was all she cared about.

"I love you, Sean," she said when their lips parted. "The stone is too large," she added inanely.

"Nothing is too large or too much for you," he told her as he pulled her closer to him.

Blair delighted in the feeling of his male strength as he carried her into the room. After he lowered her to the bed, he sat next to her.

"No more objections to another day in Mexico?" he asked.

Unwilling to trust her voice, Blair shook her head.

"Good, then we can begin our celebration now," he added, bending to uncover one peach-tipped breast. Within a heartbeat his lips covered her taut skin.

The instant his mouth touched her skin, Blair was again lost to him. As soon as their clothing was shed, their bodies became one, and their lovemaking lasted deep into the night. It was only an hour before dawn that both Blair and Sean fell into the blissful, satiated sleep of two people deeply in love. The only disturbance until they woke was Blair's dream of a beautiful blue-eyed, raven-haired woman who had locked herself away from the world to mourn her lost love over two hundred hears before.

Everything was blending together into a dreamlike fantasy for Blair. The late-afternoon sun poured through the car window, striking the brilliant emerald ring at just the right angle to create a scintillating green fire. It was an impossibility; a dream come true. But it was real, Blair decided, as she gazed out the window at the first signs of returning civilization.

Leaning her head back, Blair relaxed in the luxury and air-conditioning of the rented car, content to simply sit next to Sean. The day had been a nice and relaxing one, as she and Sean explored the Mexican countryside. They'd talked about the woman Blair had researched and driven to one of the areas that Marylena's ancestors had once owned. Before starting back, they'd had a delightful lunch in a restaurant in a small town about fifty miles outside of Mexico City.

Sean, studying Blair's profile from the corner of his eye, could not help but smile at his thoughts. Yesterday, he'd roughed out the first chapter of the Marylena-Raul story and had not been able to stop himself from picturing Blair as Marylena, even though he'd learned that the long dead woman had blue eyes, not green-flecked hazel ones.

He'd had fun doing it, and knew that as he went on with the book, he would only change Marylena's eye color and leave the rest as it was. He'd also taken the liberty of changing Marylena's name to Elaina, and the night before, when Blair had finished her story, he'd been taken completely by surprise when she told him that the original Marylena had changed her name to Elaina.

"What do you really think of Marylena Montez?" he asked Blair, breaking the silence within the car.

Blair cleared her head of her other thoughts and sat straight. She gazed at him for a moment before she spoke. "I think she was a very sad woman. She was a victim of her times and a person who had no choices in her life."

"It was the way of things in those days."

"Thank God things have changed. Sean," Blair said, her mind filled with one very important question brought on by his questions, "the man Dr. Eldridge hypnotized—Marylena's lover, who is he?"

"Then you're beginning to believe in reincarnation?" Sean asked without answering her question first.

"I don't know," she replied honestly, "there are so many unexplained things that happen. I was just curious."

"I'm sorry," Sean said. "I can't tell you."

Blair nodded, accepting his words at face value. She'd known from the beginning that Sean would not divulge that information. He'd already told her he was changing everyone's name in the book, primarily those who were alive, but in certain instances even those who were long dead, to protect the families that might still remember them.

"Can you at least tell me what kind of a man he is?"

"A man with ambitions and desires like any other," Sean whispered.

Blair stared at him, trying to interpret the strange huskiness in his voice. But by then the suburbs of Mexico City were upon them.

"When you were hypnotized, did you find a lost love?" she asked.

Sean grinned his boyish grin. "That's for me to know and for you to always wonder about. There has to be some mystery in love, doesn't there?" he asked with a raised eyebrow.

"You're not fair!" Blair pouted.

"In that case, I'll make it up to you. How about a private dinner tonight? We'll spend our last night in Mexico City having dinner on the balcony."

Blair smiled at the thought. "I'd like that."

Twenty minutes later they were in their hotel rooms. While Blair showered, Sean ordered dinner, took a quick shower and then looked over the pages of the manuscript he'd worked on the day before.

Once again he was caught within the descriptions he'd used to transfer Blair's exquisitely delicate beauty to Marylena—Elaina in the book. He didn't think Blair would mind, and he knew Marylena couldn't possibly object—not now, two hundred years after she'd died.

Then as he reread one part, a new idea formed in his mind. The idea came on the tail of a feeling that he could not ignore. He'd had this feeling before, and he could never ignore it, for it meant the birth of a new novel. He picked up a pen and began to make notes about the scene that Blair had described to him, the one where Raul and Marylena had kissed for the first time. It was the type of scene that became completely visual within his mind and was readily transposed into words.

Blair took her time in the shower, washing away the dust of the Mexican countryside. Her mind was peaceful and her thoughts calm. Yet beneath it all, she felt the hum of excitement from everything that had happened in the past few days.

Her love for Sean was a powerful force within her, and her heart soared with happiness at the merest thought of what their life together promised to be.

After leaving the shower and drying herself, Blair put on a light sundress. And an hour after they had returned to the hotel, Blair crossed her room and went through the connecting door into Sean's.

She saw Sean sitting on a chair, leaning over the small table as he wrote. She smiled when he glanced up at her and started to put the pen down.

"Don't stop because of me," she said, knowing enough about writers not to want to interrupt his train of thought.

"I'll be finished in a few minutes," he told her, thanking her with his eyes.

Blair walked past him and out onto the balcony to watch the changing colors of the sky.

Not three minutes later, Sean came onto the balcony. Stepping next to Blair, he covered her hand with his but did not speak as he watched the beauty of the sunset with her.

When the sun was gone and the sky was swathed in crimson shades, Sean took a deep breath and looked at Blair. His free hand cupped her chin gently as he lifted her face to his. "When shall we be married?"

Blair stared at him silently. She took her hand from beneath his and lifted it to caress his cheek even as a shadowy smile grew on her lips.

"You're actually asking me? I thought all your decisions about us had already been made? I mean," she continued in a teasing voice as she held out her hand to let the emerald catch whatever light it could, "anyone who would go out and buy a ring like this without asking first has all the answers, hasn't he?"

Sean cleared his throat theatrically. "Actually, I bought the ring last week in New York," Sean admitted, unable to contain the smile that framed his even white teeth.

"Oooh!" Blair spat. "You're insufferable!"

"No, I'm in love," he retorted as he reached for her.

Laughing, Blair sidestepped, but the railing prevented her from any further escape. Suddenly Sean was against her, his arms encircling her and drawing her tighter to him. Blair's laughter fled when their lips met in a passionate kiss. Heat flared instantly, and her body molded upon his. The kiss ended slowly, with Sean's lips drifting from hers to trail along her cheek and stop every second to kiss her soft skin.

"You taste so good," he murmured in a husky whisper.

Again Sean's mouth returned to Blair's, and his hands began to explore the secret places he was learning of—that they were learning of together. Each time they touched, Blair discovered more about the man she had fallen in love with. As their tongues danced, Blair knew he felt exactly the same about her—she could tell by the way he held her and the way he made love to her.

When Sean's hands slipped the straps of the sundress from her shoulders, she luxuriated in the gentle caresses that followed. She felt his desire swelling and thought she would be unable to stand upright any longer, even with the support of the railing. A low moan escaped when his fingers traced the outline of her nipple through the fabric of the dress.

Then he drew the dress down farther, and his lips took in the stiffened peak of her breast. Her hands wound into his hair urgently, even as he went to the small of her back, while his mouth rose upward, creating a trail of burning desire. Then his lips were at her ear, and she heard him speak softly.

"I've waited so long for you, my love. I need you Elaina..." The instant the word was out, Blair's body tensed, and Sean realized what had happened.

Blair froze at the sound of another's name being spoken into her ear. Her body stiffened, and her mind spun madly. She stood silently, pushing Sean away from her. Her heart tore asunder with pain.

A red, seething sheet of anger engulfed her mind, chasing away the passion and need that had been there only a heartbeat before. The rage itself helped to numb the horrible pain she felt.

Then the rage turned into a cold and calm rationality. She stared at him, a mixture of hatred and loathing suffusing her features as she raised the straps of her dress and moved out from his grasp. Her voice, when she spoke, was like an escaping hiss of steam, and she saw his eyes widen in response.

"I will never be a substitute for another," she stated, ignoring the tears that were uncontrollably winding their way down her cheeks.

"Blair," Sean said in a low voice, "let me explain."

"There's nothing to explain. I was a fool. A naive, stupid fool who trusted in you. I believed it was me you loved. But I was right about you from the very beginning, wasn't I? And you've just proven what kind of man you are.... A man I want no part of!" Blair turned to stare at the darkening panorama below.

Sean looked at her stiff back for only a second before he reacted. Reaching out, he grasped her arm and spun her to face him. "You will listen to what I have to say!" he commanded, his eyes flashing angrily, his mind burning with anger. He knew he had made a mistake, and he must get her to hear his explanation.

"Take your hands off me," she ordered, whipping her arm out of his grasp. "I won't listen to anything you have to say. I will not be lied to or decieved any longer.''

Unreasoning anger at her refusal to hear him out made Sean grab her again and pull her to him. His mouth sought hers and trapped hers completely, even though she fought him fiercely.

A split second after his lips met hers, a flame leapt to life within her, fighting her own will to be free again. He held her so tight that she could hardly breathe or battle against his strength. His mouth was merciless. Beneath his questing lips, her body began to betray her once again as it responded to the man who held her trapped to him. She tried to keep up her fight but could not.

The instant her body relaxed, Sean pulled his mouth from hers. ''You can't fight it, Blair. Even if you want to, your body and heart tell me the truth. You are mine. You have been since the beginning!'' he stated, releasing her when the last word was said.

Stepping back, Blair took a deep, shuddering breath and clasped her hands together before her. As she stared at him, her fingers worked upon the ring. When she saw him start to reach for her again, Blair willed her arm to obey her commands; her arm whipped up and her palm met the side of his face.

The sound of the slap echoed in the night, and she saw Sean go stiff. She watched in morbid fascination as a vein began to pulse in his cheek. ''Did you think you could buy my love?'' she asked seethingly as she extended her hand, the engagement ring resting in the exact center of her palm.

She saw, as he took the ring from her, that the vein in his cheek now throbbed wildly. They faced each other across the space of eternity until Blair stepped past him and went inside.

After locking the connecting door, Blair went to the phone. The tears she'd shed had dried on her face, and she refused to give in to them anymore. Once again she had learned one of life's lessons, and the pain that accompanied it was almost too much to bear.

She asked the operator to connect her with the airlines, and then learned that there was enough time for her to catch the last direct flight to New York.

She checked out of the hotel twenty-five minutes later and went to the airport. There she sat in the waiting area, staring vacantly out at the runways until her flight was announced and she was able to board the plane.

Once the plane was airborne, and as the lights of Mexico City faded into obscurity, Blair closed her eyes in an effort to banish Sean's face from her mind.

She tried to ignore the bold glint that had always been present in his deep eyes; she willed herself not to see the sensuous curve of his mouth or feel the wondrously gentle touch of his hands.

In time, she told herself, *in time.*

Chapter Ten

"Alice Daniels on line two." Blair looked up as her assistant's voice issued from the intercom. Shrugging uncertainly, Blair stared at the telephone receiver. She had spoken to Alice on the phone only twice in the four weeks she'd been back. The first time was to tell Alice that she never wanted to see Sean again, the second was to tell her the research was done.

"'Morning," Blair said when she picked up the phone.

"You've been avoiding me again," Alice charged in her studiously aloof voice.

"I've been working."

"And avoiding me.... I know you are, but I'll accept that for now. I'm calling to compliment you and thank you for the work you did for Sean. And especially for finishing so quickly."

"You're welcome," Blair said, trying to maintain the same type of businesslike aloofness that Alice used so well.

"You can't match me, Blair. I was born to this business. Besides," Alice said, her voice growing warmer, "I love you, and I know you're hurting."

"Please, Alice, I have to work this out by myself this time. It's...it's different."

"After what you've already told me, I know that. But I also wanted you to know that you'll always have my shoulder to lean on. Sean may be my client, but *you* are my friend."

The iron control she'd forced on herself loosened as Alice talked, and Blair realized she did not have to be afraid to speak with her friend.

"I have a late date tonight—an after-dinner date," Alice said mysteriously. "How about dinner?"

"Sure," Blair decided, suddenly wanting to have company for a change. "I'll be finished here around five-thirty. Where do you want to meet?"

"Marrebello's. I'll be waiting," Alice stated as she hung up.

"'Bye," Blair said to the dial tone. But she felt better knowing that she would see her friend tonight for the first time since returning from Mexico City. *Has it really been a month since I left Mexico?*

The day she'd returned she'd written her report on Marylena Montez and sent it to Alice. The next day she'd left to continue the research in Boston. Blair had taken Laura with her, and from Boston they'd flown to Tennessee to work on the last case history. She knew she had taken Laura for two distinctly different reasons; one was to help complete the research on time, the other was as protection in case Sean decided to follow her again.

Blair had also made it a habit while they were away to register at the hotel in Laura's name only. It was always Laura who answered the phone and screened any of Blair's calls. In that, she'd believed she'd had no choice. From the moment she'd arrived in New York, Sean had called constantly.

She'd spoken to him only one time without hanging up, and that had been shortly after she'd returned from Tennessee. He had tried to explain what had happened, and Blair had again cut him off, using similar words that he himself had used that terrible night on the Delaware.

"Sean, you're an excellent writer. A true professional. But from this moment on the only thing we will share is business, and only for this book!"

"My memory," he told her, "for what I've written or said is quite good, and a little plagiarism has never hurt me before. Just remember, Blair, the moment I set eyes on you, *you* became my business."

"In that case," Blair retorted bitterly, "I suggest you find a new venture, because you've bankrupted this one!" Angrily, she'd begun to hang up the phone, but before the receiver had reached its cradle, she'd heard his voice float up.

"You love me," he'd said.

Slowly, Blair had completed her motion and hung up the telephone. He'd only called once more after that, and Blair had hung up the moment she'd heard his voice.

He's right, Blair thought as she willed her mind out of the past. *I do love him.*

Closing her eyes, Blair forced herself to banish Sean from invading her every thought. To help her free her mind of him, she took the top file folder from the ever increasing pile on her desk and opened it. Looking at Laura's notations, Blair tried to decipher exactly what the author required in the way of research.

Fifteen minutes later she was still trying to get through the same page. In spite of her concerted efforts the words swam in fuzzy circles. Blair was still in a haze, living with the misty feelings that had held her prisoner ever since she'd finished the research for Sean.

Until she'd actually completed the assignment, she had been unable to manage competently by burying herself within her work so that she would not have to think of him. But when the final page of Sean's report had been typed and sent out, she no longer had her anger to goad her on. The realization that it was over had combined with the knowledge that she would have no more contact with Sean, and her loss had grown into an acute and painful ache that stayed with her every day.

This has to stop, she told herself as she surveyed her office for the umpteenth time that day. *Where is my energy? What happened to my drive,* she asked herself sadly.

Once again, and very much unwanted, Sean's tauntingly confident smile and deeply intense eyes rose up before her. "Go away!" she commanded. Turning, Blair looked at the jumble of paperwork on her desk and suddenly knew that she had to take some time off and get her emotions repaired. She knew she had to get away for a while.

Blair pressed the intercom and called her assistants into the office. Once Laura and Stephanie were seated, she wasted no time.

"I'm going to take some time off," she informed them, "and I want the two of you to handle everything until I get back. And I mean everything! Laura, you take care of the Simm's project. Stephanie, you work on Warner's first and then on Rheinhart's."

Both women looked at their boss with duplicate expressions of incredulity, not sure that they had really heard her correctly. Blair knew she had handed them a surprise with her announcement: Blair had not taken a single vacation since she'd started the business.

"How long will you be gone?" Laura finally asked.

"I'm not sure. But I'll check in frequently. If anything important crops up while I'm gone, decide on whether or not the two of you can handle it. If not, turn it down."

"Blair, are you sure?" Laura asked quickly.

Blair shook her head. "The only thing I'm sure about is that I need to get away. I'll clean up my desk today, take care of petty cash and set up the payroll for the next few weeks. Now," she said with a tentative smile to the two women, "get out of here and go back to work."

Both women rose and left, but Blair did not miss the concerned look that Laura cast toward her as she closed Blair's door.

Entering the dimness of Marrebello's, one of the publishing world's more fashionable eating and meeting places, Blair was immediately immersed in the after-work crowd overflowing the bar area. She spotted many familiar faces and returned every smile of recognition with one of her own.

The coolness of the air-conditioning was welcome after her walk in the hot June streets, but she could have done without the crush of people who now surrounded her. Blair maintained her tenuous smile as she fought through the milling crowd and made her way toward the dining section.

As she walked, she was aware of the beauty of the decor. The long, dark wood bar, accented by brass fixtures, looked the perfect counterpoint to the people who stood at it: it was conservative but elegant, as were the publishing executives themselves. Hundreds of glasses hung suspended from ceiling racks, adding an effective touch to the room's look.

Finally, just when she thought she would never get through the crowd, she entered the more spacious and less crowded dining area. Pausing for a moment to look around, Blair spotted Alice's blond head and walked past two dessert carts filled with Italian pastries. Alice's greeting was an open and friendly smile.

"Your drink madame," Alice said, pointing to a glass filled with amber liquid.

Sitting, Blair placed her purse on an empty chair and lifted the glass to her lips. After she sipped, she nodded approvingly at the fruity taste of the aperitif. With a sigh, she sat back.

"My, we certainly are talkative tonight," Alice offered.

"I'm sure we will be eventually...if I know you," Blair retorted in a good-natured way. "Are you hungry?"

"I can eat."

"Good, because tonight I'm starting a long overdue vacation, and I'm going to make a pig of myself!" Blair declared.

Alice's only response was to raise her eyebrows. Almost on cue with her action, the waiter appeared with the menus.

Blair opened her menu immediately and, scanning the contents, decided on what she would have. When she lifted her eyes, she saw the waiter had disappeared.

"Patience," Alice remarked at her expression, "he'll be back. Why are you doing this? When I'm depressed I can't eat a thing. No one does," Alice stated knowledgeably.

"I'm not no one. I eat when I'm depressed. Alice, I...I just don't give a damn," she finally admitted.

"Sure," Alice said dryly. Then she neatly changed the subject. "Where are you going on this vacation of yours?"

"I haven't gotten that far yet," Blair confessed. After Alice gave her an I-knew-it kind of look, Blair saw her friend's eyes turn distant.

"I just thought of something," Alice muttered as she stood. "I have to make a phone call."

Before Blair could say anything, Alice was gone. She returned five minutes later with a satisfied smile on her lips. The waiter eventually came back to the table and asked for their order.

Blair ordered first. "Shrimp cocktail with lots of sauce. Then I'll have veal cordon bleu, steamed green beans, a baked potato, salad and...I'll think about dessert later."

Alice ordered veal scallopini and a small green salad. When the waiter left, Alice told Blair that her order wasn't really that fattening after all.

"That was just a warm up," Blair countered, her face set in serious lines. "I saw the dessert carts on my way in. Now, what was that phone call about?"

"Paranoid, aren't we?"

"No, I just know you, remember?"

"Sometimes.... But if you're interested, I've found a great place for your vacation."

"Really? I suppose you've already made reservations for me at a romantic little inn on a bank of the Delaware River. Somewhere near the New York-Pennsylvania border perhaps?" Blair remarked with not a little sarcasm.

Alice shook her head and sighed loudly at Blair's words. "Take that look off your face, and I'll pretend I didn't hear what you just said. You've heard of George Marks, haven't you?"

"Of course I have. He's a leading historian and author. His books on American history have all been highly acclaimed."

"George is a friend of mine, not a client. He has a lovely house in Charleston, which he only uses in the fall when he's lecturing at the university. And..."

"Try not to be a salesperson. Just tell me what you've arranged," Blair interrupted. From years of experience, she knew that when Alice started to prattle, she was usually trying to convince Blair to accept one of her ideas that she had already made a commitment on.

Alice sighed resignedly. "Just because you're depressed doesn't mean you can't let me have my fun. I really had a nice surprise all worked out for you. And in record time! How about showing some appreciation? Anyway, I—"

"George Marks isn't another pseudonym, for—"

"Stop it! No, it's not and I said I wouldn't discuss Sean tonight, didn't I?"

Blair nodded guiltily, thinking that perhaps Alice was right and she was getting paranoid.

"May I finish now?" Alice asked testily.

Blair nodded again.

"I called George," she began from where she'd left off, "and he said the house is available and that you could stay there for as long as you wanted."

"Really?" Blair asked, her voice growing excited. The memory of one previous and short visit to Charleston paraded through her head. "Where is the house?"

"I'm not really sure. Somewhere in the historic section, I believe."

"Mmmm," Blair added in a noncommittal way as the waiter placed her appetizer before her. Just looking at the large shrimp made Blair's mouth water. Ignoring Alice, Blair started to eat.

"May I?" Alice asked, her fork already hovering above the dish.

"One," Blair stated and smiled when Alice frowned. "I'm depressed so I'm eating. You, my friend, on the other hand, are full of life and joy and are watching your figure so that Halston you're wearing will still fit when you meet your date later."

"Shrimp aren't fattening," Alice defended as she took a shrimp and dipped it into the spicy sauce. She ate it slowly, savoring each bite. This too had been a game they played frequently over the years. Alice would always order light, and then steal some of Blair's.

Blair finished the three remaining shrimp in short order and smiled her satisfaction. "Okay," she said.

"Okay the shrimp?"

"Okay the house. I'll take it."

"Good. Oh, yes, since you were the one who mentioned it first, I also have your check with me," Alice told her.

"Mentioned what first? And what check?"

"Sean. And Sean's check."

Blair's stomach twisted, but she fought back against the sudden sensation of her loss. "Send it to the office; they'll deposit it."

"He asked me to give it to you personally," Alice replied just as the waiter returned and placed their food on the table.

Blair's veal looked wonderful. A crisp layer of golden breading peaked out beneath artfully placed brown mushroom sauce. The string beans looked bright and crisp next to the veal, and Blair, with a malicious look aimed at her friend, dumped three pats of butter into the steaming baked potato and nodded to the serving boy who was approaching with a silver serving cup of sour cream.

Blair continued to watch Alice's horrified gaze as she asked for a second scoop of the white cream. With a nod to Alice, she dug her fork deep into the potato.

"You're certainly not going to have to worry about *any* man if you eat like that for another week," Alice warned.

"Exactly," Blair agreed through a mouthful of potato. By the time they finished the main course, Blair thought her stomach would explode if anything else were to pass her lips. She declined the dessert cart, but accepted the cup of coffee placed before her.

Alice, looking at her through lowered lids, smiled. "I guess you aren't that depressed if you're skipping dessert."

"The check?" she reminded Alice.

"If you're not going into the office tomorrow, why don't you endorse the check to me, and I'll send one of my own to your office?" Alice volunteered as she reached for her purse and withdrew a slim envelope.

As she did, Blair delved into her own purse and took out a pen. Then she took the envelope from Alice and slowly opened it and withdrew the check. Her heart pounded loudly when she saw Sean's bold signature. *Just like him,* she thought, *bold and insufferable.* When she looked at the line where the amount was written, she froze. She stared at it for a long moment before she looked at the rest of the check.

Blair lifted her head quickly and looked around for the waiter. When she spotted him, she raised her arm and called him over. She ignored Alice's perplexed features while she waited and, when the waiter arrived, Blair smiled at him. "Chocolate mousse, please," she said.

"Blair!" Alice cried in alarm.

"And you, my friend," Blair said, fixing Alice with a penetrating stare, "can give this check back to *Mr. Mathias* and tell him to...to... That I will *only* accept the fee we agreed upon. Alice...how could you?"

"How could I what? What did he do now?" she asked in a strangely subdued whisper.

Rather than explain, Blair handed Alice the check and watched as her friend's expression went from bewilderment to surprise. When the mousse arrived in its silver cup, Blair picked up the spoon and took a large scoop.

"He does love you," Alice said as she let out a low laugh. Then she blanched. "How can you possibly eat any more?"

Blair paused, the second spoonful almost at her lips. "Easily. And don't tell me he loves me. He doesn't! He loves someone named Elaina."

"Wow, this is not only going to become the classic literary story of the decade—it's going to keep me in lunches for a year," Alice stated as she picked up her own spoon and helped herself to some of the chocolate mousse. "Good," she commented.

"Alice, if you dare tell anyone about this..." she warned, snatching the check from her friend's hand as she spoke. She read the printing on the check, as she absently ate yet another spoonful of mousse.

"A lover's check," she read aloud. Then she skipped the place where her name was written and went on to the amount. "Good for one marriage. Payable upon presentation."

Blair licked the spoon thoughtfully before putting it down. Her hazel eyes locked on Alice's blue ones for a long drawn-out moment.

"You tell your client that if I don't receive my full fee within the next three days, I will take him to court." When she finished speaking, Blair lifted the still half-filled dish of mousse and upended it on top of the check.

"Blair!"

"I'll call you in the morning and get all the information about the house in Charleston," she said as she rose. But before she walked away, she looked back down at Alice, who was trying to control her laughter. "Oh, until your client pays his bill, the dinner is on you."

With that, Blair walked away, aware not only of Alice's laughter following her but of the glances from the other people in the room. Yet surmounting all the activity was the dull ache in her heart.

Sean stood on the bank of the Delaware, his eyes vacant, his mind churning with myriad thoughts. Ever since that night in Mexico City when he'd foolishly spoken a name he had no right to speak, he'd been trying to make Blair listen to reason.

Although he knew it was a simple mistake brought on by his own compulsive need to work when ideas formed, he should never have said what he did—he had never done anything like that before.

Blair could have no way of knowing that Elaina was but a character in a book and a woman who had been dead for over two hundred years.

It's over, Sean told himself. It had been, he'd realized, when he'd finally spoken to her two weeks ago and she'd told him off in no uncertain terms.

Suddenly Sean could not accept his own thoughts and knew that no matter what happened he could not let her go. He loved her, and he knew that she loved him. *But how do I make her see that too?*

"I will, somehow I will," he told the dark rushing waters that reflected the small sliver of the sickle moon above.

Charleston and the house Blair was staying at were truly the perfect escape from reality. The vast difference in her surroundings contributed more to the uplifting of her spirits than she had thought possible. The fresh and clean air blowing in from Charleston Harbor through the open multi-paned double windows of the bedroom had a marvelously cleansing effect on her mind.

The varied scents of the flowers and trees abounding in the air aroused her senses as no perfume could. The sunlight, pouring in its welcome, filtering seductively through the gauzy curtains, pleaded with Blair to welcome the day. And today was the first day of the rest of her life. As Blair thought of the old saying, she knew that on this day she would start to rebuild what Sean Mathias had destroyed.

The night before, Blair had arrived from the airport and the taxi had driven into a different era. Through the taxi windows she had watched the modern buildings and contemporary shopping malls disappear, replaced by older and more sedate and beautiful homes, buildings and mansions.

When the driver had pulled to a stop in front of a large, four-columned house facing the Battery at the very tip of Charleston, Blair was hard pressed to believe her good fortune. The house itself was of another age, restored perfectly, and looking very much as she imagined it would have in the early 1800s. Blair could almost picture liveried servants running about, serving drinks from silver trays to guests who wore fabulous gowns and stylish longcoats and breeches.

Stepping from the cab, Blair had taken several bills from her wallet and handed them to the driver. As she had, she'd noticed the large mahogany door open, and in the gentle light that spilled from the doorway, she'd seen two people. By the time the driver had deposited her suitcases on the narrow sidewalk, a man and woman in their early sixties had come up to her.

"Miss Sanders?" The man had asked in a pleasant southern accent.

"Yes," she'd said as she looked at him. His white hair was combed back neatly and his blue eyes held hers steadily.

"Welcome to Charleston. I'm Andrew Hadley, the caretaker, and this is my wife Claire, who is Mr. Marks's housekeeper," he'd stated as he lifted her two suitcases and led her into the house.

Once inside, Mr. Hadley had taken her things upstairs while Mrs. Hadley, a stout woman of medium height had given Blair a tour of the house.

And what a house it was, Blair had discovered as she'd walked on the highly varnished parquet floors. The large interior rooms had been completely renovated. Looking around everywhere, Blair had realized that everything was an exact replica of what the house must have looked like after it was first built.

While escorting Blair through the house, Mrs. Hadley had echoed Blair's thoughts while she'd proudly told Blair in great detail the house's history.

By the time Blair had reached the bedroom she would be using, she had become filled with the wonder of George Marks's home. When she'd entered the bedroom, her heart had skipped a beat—the room was decorated all in white. Gauze curtains hung on two sets of double windows, the walls were a soft white shade and even the ornately handcrafted dresser had a highly lacquered white finish. In the center of the room on a white-dyed rice carpet stood a large, dark walnut four-poster canopied bed; white mosquito netting encased it like a cocoon.

"It's lovely," Blair had finally whispered to Mrs. Hadley after drinking her fill of the room.

The housekeeper had beamed at Blair's approval. "It is. And Mr. Marks had it redone to look just like the summer bedrooms of the wealthy people of those past times." Then Mrs. Hadley had begun to unpack Blair's suitcases.

Although Blair had protested that she would unpack herself, the older woman had shaken her head and told her that it was part of her job.

Later that night just before Blair had gone to bed, Mrs. Hadley had come into her room carrying a silver tea service. She'd placed it on the white wrought-iron table and smiled. "Breakfast will be whenever you wake. Just come downstairs and tell me what you'd like to have." Then she had left to allow Blair her privacy before going to bed.

As the memory of her arrival faded from her thoughts, Blair decided that it was time to leave the bed and begin the day...and her new life. But before she could get up, a fragment of the dream she'd had the previous night returned with an all too sudden clarity.

It was night time. She was walking along a beach hand in hand with Sean. A crescent moon hung in the sky above them, and the soft sounds of waves lapping at the sands gave the couple a calm sense of oneness. They stopped and began to kiss. Moments later they were lying upon the sand, moving gently as their bodies joined in a ritual as old as time itself.

With a shiver Blair chased away the memory of the dream and did her best to hold back the waves of sadness the mere thought of Sean brought out in her. Bringing forth her resolve to forget the man she loved, Blair brushed aside the mosquito netting and left the bed. She was wearing a long white nightgown, and smiled at how its color blended so perfectly with the room. Walking to the windows, Blair parted the curtains and gazed out on the waters of Charleston Harbor. Because the house stood on the corner of Church Street and South Battery, the second-story window opened to an unrestricted view of the eastern waters.

Blair drank in the way the rising sun sent sparkling lances to blaze along the tips of the gentle blue-green swells, making her long for the talent to capture the scene on canvas. Finally, after her eyes had feasted upon the morning's grace for long enough, Blair left the window to prepare for the day.

Forty minutes later, dressed in khaki Bermuda shorts, a matching safari top and leather sandals, Blair descended the wide curving stairway to the main floor. Halfway down she paused, almost believing that Clark Gable would appear any instant to smile up to her. Laughing at her silliness, Blair shook away the image of Rhett Butler and continued down.

In the large main hallway, Blair turned toward the kitchen, following the aroma of freshly brewed coffee that made her mouth water.

In the old-style kitchen, with its cast-iron stove and racks of hanging copper pots, Blair found Mrs. Hadley at work by a thick butcher-block table.

"Good morning," Blair said.

"'Mornin', ma'am," Mrs. Hadley replied in a cheerful southern drawl. "Hope ya'll slept well."

"Like a baby," Blair replied. "And the coffee smells delicious," she added.

"'Course it is," the housekeeper stated proudly. "I grind the beans myself, and add just the right amount of chicory to mellow out the taste. Would you like some eggs?"

For some reason, the thought of food became unappealing and she shook her head. "No, thank you, just coffee," she told the housekeeper as she walked to the highly polished kitchen table.

"I've set the table on the piazza for you." Mrs. Hadley smiled then. "That's the terrace to you Yankees," she added good-naturedly. "It's just through those doors," she said, pointing a flour-spotted finger in the right direction.

Nodding, Blair turned and walked out into the gentle heat of the southern morning. The sun's warm rays combined with the seaport's mild humidity beckoned her seductively. Sitting at a glass-topped wrought-iron table shaded by a large magnolia tree, Blair picked up the newspaper that had been thoughtfully placed there. As her body and spirits began to absorb the gentle and relaxing heat of the day, Blair glanced at the headlines but found nothing of interest. When she put the paper down, she saw that Mrs. Hadley had arrived at the table.

The housekeeper poured dark, steaming coffee from a glass carafe and then placed the carafe on a candle warmer. Then, with an expression that bore no argument, she put a napkin-covered basket on the table next to a dish of soft butter and a container of jam.

"I made the muffins this morning. Blueberry," she declared as she turned and strode regally from the piazza.

Blair stared at the basket and then back at her single place setting. *It should be for two,* she thought. Then she lifted the cup of rich smelling coffee. Before she could take her first sip, Sean's haunting image appeared before her.

"Damn you!" she whispered. Willing the vision away, Blair took her first sip of coffee. Her eyebrows rose in silent appreciation of the drink, which had a rich taste that was unique as well as delicious.

Suddenly, her appetite returned, and she reached into the basket to retrieve one oven-hot muffin. Breaking it in half, Blair spread a little butter on it. Then, with a smile of remembrance of her dinner with Alice several nights before, she added a large dollop of jam and bit into the muffin. Blair ate two muffins before she realized she was full.

Over her second cup of coffee Blair tried to plan out her day. Nothing this morning, she decided, but later she would walk through the narrow streets and look at the restored historic homes.

Just as the sun rose, Sean arrived at the hotel where he'd already reserved a room. After registering and unpacking his suitcase, he returned to the lobby and went into the coffee shop for a light breakfast.

By seven-thirty he was standing in the park, looking at the large, four-columned white house across the boulevard and waiting for Blair to come out.

He had decided that he had to try one more time to get past Blair's protective barriers and make her listen to his explanation. All his life Sean had gone after what he wanted, and he was not about to stop now.

But he'd also decided that he would not pursue Blair any further if, after she heard what he had to say, she still refused to make a life with him. In that case he would leave her to herself forever.

Yet Sean believed in himself and was sure that once he talked with her she would understand. That was why he had coerced Alice into telling him where Blair had fled to, and then made Alice the promises he had.

Come to me, Blair, he called silently.

Outside the house, Blair went down the five stone steps and traversed the cobblestone walk to the sidewalk. Earlier, from her window, she had seen a small park across the main street. She decided now that she wanted to visit it.

Moments later she wandered through the park until she reached the cement walkway that was part of the balustrade overhanging the water. Leaning on the cement abutment, Blair watched the boats and ships weaving their way along the horizon. To her right was a land mass called James Island; to her left was the ever present reminder of the Civil War, Fort Sumter.

After several minutes of relaxed gazing, Blair went to one of the many benches lining the walk. Choosing an unoccupied bench that still afforded her a view, Blair sank down and closed her eyes for a moment.

Here, far away from New York and everyone she was familiar with, Blair was able to let her barriers down and set her emotions free. Slowly, she went on a deep and introspective voyage in an effort to understand what had happened to her and to see if she could find whatever strength was necessary for her to pull her life together again.

Blair forced herself to admit once again the depth of her love for Sean. She hadn't known him for a very long time, and everything had happend so quickly, but her heart told her mind the truth as it felt it was.

Never before in her life, not even with Brian, had she reacted to a man the way she had to Sean. Just a glance from his simmering eyes had been enough to send shivers racing through her. When he touched her, desire sprang forth boldly.

Blair understood that her feeling for Sean in no way tarnished or hurt her memory and love for Brian. Her love for each man was different, just as Brian had been different from Sean. *Brian is gone,* Blair reminded herself as she opened her eyes. Yet the memory of his always gentle love rose up to comfort her in this time of sadness, to ease her tormented thoughts for a moment.

From the corner of her eye, Blair saw a person move to the other side of the bench and settle down there. Ignoring the newcomer, Blair closed her eyes again and let her thoughts take over.

Was I wrong? Or am I just afraid I'm not woman enough to tame Sean's restlessness? Or was it, she wondered, that she thought herself inadequate to handle competition from another woman? Or was what she felt justified anger and outright disgust at being made love to and then being called by another's name? But the more Blair pondered her own questions, the more confused she became.

"Don't you wish all the days were as beautiful as this?" asked the man who had sat down near her. Without opening her eyes, Blair nodded.

Then, as slowly as water seeping through an old thatched roof, the sound of the man's voice penetrated into every level of her mind. With a sensation that was a cross between pure rage and unexpected joy, Blair opened her eyes.

Turning her head slowly, she found herself staring at Sean, who was returning her wide-eyed look of disbelief with his irritatingly impudent smile.

Not again, she cried silently.

Chapter Eleven

At least this time you're not wearing a disguise. Go away," she snapped, "go back to Elaina!"

Sean remained silent, but Blair saw his hand move to the pocket of his white sport shirt, his bronzed fingers dipping within for a moment before reappearing with a folded slip of gray paper.

Sean stared at her openly, his thoughts racing. Through the strength of his willpower, he held back the things he wanted to say while he drank his fill of her beauty, made so intriguing by the morning sun. He had been waiting for two hours for this opportunity, and knew that a few more moments of silence would not hurt him.

"If I'm not mistaken, I was informed that I had only three days to render full payment *in the correct amount*, before you took me to court. Here," he said, extending the check to her.

Blair took the piece of paper as if it were a flame, holding it gingerly between thumb and forefinger while she continued to stare at him.

"You could have mailed it."

"And taken the chance that the mails would be late? You know how undependable the post office has become."

"How did you find me? No, don't bother. It was Alice. Again!" she stated accusatorily.

"A writer should also be a good detective. But I'll tell you that it wasn't easy this time. I had to blackmail Alice," he said with another smile.

"I'm sure you did just that," Blair retorted, her every word dripping with sarcasm. "But now that you've fulfilled your *obligation*, Mr. Mathias, I'll thank you to leave me alone."

"No," Sean whispered as the smile left his face. His eyes changed into burning orbs, and his resolve grew in direct proportion to her words. "No," he repeated.

Blair's hands clenched as she fought the sudden need to touch him. It was a desire that came close to overwhelming her. Her heart began to pound, and her stomach knotted painfully. *No,* she told herself, *this is wrong. This can't happen again!* Afraid of trusting herself to answer him, Blair started to rise from the bench. Before she was three inches off the cement-and-wood seat, Sean's fingers encircled her arm and pulled her back onto the bench.

"Leave me alone!" she whispered heatedly, the words barely audible as they escaped from her unyielding lips.

"I won't let you run away again," he stated in a determined voice.

"I'll do as I damn well please. Let go of my arm!"

"I know you'll do as you *please*. I just want you to make sure that what you do pleases you, not hurts you," he told her as he leaned toward her.

"You hurt me. Let me go, Sean," Blair pleaded, watching helplessly while his face grew near.

"Will you talk this out with me?" he asked.

"No."

Sean stared at her stoney features for a moment longer. Then he slowly shook his head but did not release her arm. "It's hard to be in love with a woman who believes she's been wronged and who thinks the person who wronged her can do no right. Talk to me, Blair. Listen to what I have to say." Then he took his hand from her arm.

As Blair gazed into Sean's eyes, his words reached into the very depths of her heart and mind even as she felt him pull away from her. His words affected her deeply, and she even thought she heard a glimmer of truth within them. When her arm was free, she glanced down and saw that his fingers had left bright red marks on her skin. Refusing to meet his eyes, Blair looked away, absently rubbing her arm.

"All right," she half whispered a moment later.

Sean continued to study Blair's profile and saw the moisture filming her eyes. Reaching out, he cupped her chin and turned her face to his. He wanted to see her whole face. He needed to look deep into her eyes before he spoke. "Walk with me?" he asked.

Blair could only nod. She stood when he did, feeling defenseless and in a strange trancelike state that made her unable to resist his request. They went slowly to the cement balustrade and then began to move along the walk.

"I came here to get away from you. Why can't I?" she asked.

"Because I can't let you do that."

"I really didn't want to see you again."

"I know," he said.

Blair turned to look at him, surprised by his admission. Before she could say more, he continued to speak.

"I know that you *think* you didn't want to see me again, but no matter how I try to convince myself of that, I can't believe it's true." When Sean stopped, he looked skyward, his eyes following the path of a black-spotted sea gull.

There were so many things he wanted to say to her and so many things he needed to make her understand. When the sea gull swooped close to him, Sean spoke again.

"I've already told you how much I want you. I gave you all the commitments you asked for, and in return I found my hands filled with an hysterical, jealous woman who didn't have the decency or the courtesy to stay around long enough to listen to reason!"

His sharp-edged words took Blair by surprise. But at the same time, his attack helped to let her find her own anger, and with that her strength returned.

"I only followed the example I was shown," she flung back in challenge, reminding him of his own actions that long ago night at his house.

"But you only learned half the lesson. Or did you forget that I came back to you the first time?"

"I haven't forgotten a thing! I've always listened to reason," she stated, holding his deep brown eyes with her lighter ones. "But in this case, the explanation was all too obvious," she finished, her words once again weighted by sarcasm.

"Perhaps on the surface what happened would appear cut and dried."

"As a professional researcher," she said, her voice taking on a patient quality which she did not feel, "I'm becoming very curious to hear you explain this Elaina to me." Tensing, Blair looked at him in direct challenge as she did her best to ignore the sudden onset of doubts that rose up to plague her while she waited for him to tell his story.

Sean put his hand lightly on Blair's shoulder, the need to touch her growing strong. "I came prepared to explain everything to you, but I was hoping, stupidly it seems, that there would be no need for explanations. I was under the mistaken impression that the love we had...have should be enough to keep us together. I believed the love we discovered included trust and faith in each other."

Blair swallowed tightly while his words reverberated over and over again within her mind. Her heart began to race. *Oh, how I want his words to be true,* she thought. She needed them to be, but in the back of her mind she could still feel his lips on her skin as he murmured the other woman's name.

"You..." she began, but had to stop to moisten her lips with her tongue. "You said you loved me, and I wanted to believe that because I love you. But I..." Blair could not finish her words, because the dreadful pain of his deception had again risen to lash fiercely at her.

Sean stared at her, silently pleading with her to go on, but finally, when he realized that she would not, he took a deep breath. He had come prepared to tell her what had happened that night in Mexico City. But when he looked into the pained depths of her eyes, he knew that to admit his mistake and the reason for it, might hurt her just as much as if there had been another woman.

How can I tell her that I called her by the name I had given her in the book? How can I make her understand that when I spoke Elaina's name, it was hers. Sean realized that if he explained the truth about that night, Blair would most probably not believe him. He didn't think she'd be able to accept the fact that he had been working on his book, making detailed notes of a love scene between Elaina and Raul, and because he had given Blair's features and beauty to Elaina he had foolishly whispered Elaina's name.

Sean was certain that Blair would then think that he had a need to fantasize about another woman when he was with her, a woman that he alone had created.

All these thoughts had taken but an instant in time, and as they raced through Sean's head, he saw that Blair was still staring at him. Finally, unhappy with what he was about to do, yet knowing intuitively that he must convince her of his love, he began to speak.

His eyes swept across Blair's face, and suddenly Sean changed his mind about what he would tell her. "Would you believe me if I said that there was no Elaina?"

"Are you telling me she was a figment of your imagination? Please, Sean, I expect better than that from you."

Sean exhaled slowly. "Elaina is a figment of...of the past," he said, giving voice to the lie he had tried to avoid, a lie that he had been doomed, he knew all along, to put into words.

"And, Blair, Elaina is no longer a part of my life."

Blair suddenly found herself wanting desperately to believe him so that her heart would stop torturing her so mercilessly; but the logical part of her mind would not allow her that relief.

"I don't love Elaina, no matter what you might think. She is not my lover, Blair."

Blair tried not to hear him, tried not to listen or to believe him, but she suddenly felt his words within her heart, her breath catching at his last statement. "I want to believe that, Sean, I want to very badly," she admitted honestly.

Sean almost threw his hands into the air in frustration, but again, his own inner strengths would not let him give up now. "I've never asked you about Brian. I never asked if you still loved him, I just assumed you did and that you always will. I'm realistic enough to understand that people can love the memory of someone who is gone from them, while they give a new love to the person whom they share their present life with. Am I so wrong?" he asked, his eyes never once leaving hers.

Sean's words tunneled deeply into Blair's mind, forcing her to think hard about what he had said. An instant later she knew he was right. Her love for Brian was still a part of her but it did not alter or interfere with her ability to love Sean completely.

Blair wanted to tell him that, to admit that she loved him deeply, but all the uncertainties of their times together and the deceit she had felt so acutely made her continue to doubt him.

"Why? Why do you want me?" she asked, taking a deep breath as she spoke.

Sean laughed, but it was not the clear, free laughter that was so much a part of him. "I don't think anyone has a choice about who they fall in love with, not if it really is love," he told her.

Then Sean drew her slowly to him, and Blair watched as the sun was blocked by his face a moment before his lips touched hers. And then Blair tasted the magic of his lips once again after so long a time without him. The hammering of her heart increased its rhythm, and the fire that was growing upon her lips spread downward into her body. When they parted, it was too soon, and all of Blair's hard-fought resolve crumpled beneath the power of that one small kiss.

"What you must believe, my love, is that there is only you in my life," Sean stated.

"I want to Sean, but I can't forget either," she whispered when she found her voice.

"I don't expect you to forget, just to accept the fact that I love only you."

"I need some time," she said as she gazed into the unending depths of his eyes.

"I won't rush you this time. Take as much time as you need, but," he said, his eyes sparkling brilliantly as the corners of his mouth turned up, "you're going to spend that time with me."

"I'm staying for at least a week, possibly longer," she told him quickly.

"I can write wherever I am," he countered.

Blair shrugged. "Not if you're with me all the time."

"True," Sean admitted. "But you don't know my writing habits that well either. And what I'm working on now, I don't need to spend full days with. I expect to be working every morning until at least noon. And while we're in Charleston, I plan on having every afternoon and evening free so that I can pay court to you!"

His last words caught her by surprise. "Is that what you're planning to do? Court me?" Slipping from beneath his hands, Blair whirled away, a brilliant smile lighting up her face for a split second before her features turned serious again.

I can't take this chance. I can't be hurt again, she told herself. *Why do I love him so much?* And her love for him was so strong a force within her that the harder she tried to make herself not want to take another chance, the more she found herself wanting to.

"At least you still have your sense of humor," she said, giving him a quick shake of her head. "I have to admit that you could not have picked a better place for courting," she said as she pointed toward the old and romantic mansions lining the boulevard across from the park.

"My thoughts exactly," Sean agreed. "I will make love to you under the stars and moon: I will carry you about in a horse-drawn carriage and take you wherever your heart decrees," he proclaimed in a theatrical voice and manner. But even as he spoke so lightly, he saw Blair's face grow tense once again. "What?" he asked.

"I have no intention of picking up our relationship at the same point where we left off. Don't expect me to grace your bed or any other place where you might decide to try to make love to me," she informed him in cool tones, letting the determination within her mind lace her words. *He won't hurt me again,* she promised herself.

Astonishingly, Blair watched Sean throw back his head and laugh deeply. For just an instant, while he stood beneath the golden rays of the sun and his powerful body was outlined by its shimmering light, Sean looked like a mythological deity. Her heart skipped a beat, and her mouth was suddenly dry.

"Literary license, Blair," he mananged to say through his laughter. "Making love to you under the moon doesn't necessarily mean the physical act itself. Looking into your eyes is one way of making love; holding your hand is another. Caressing your cheek with my fingers is as much a part of lovemaking as..."

"No more," Blair pleaded, shivering at the memories his words brought up in her mind. "I'll accept what you said."

"I am making progress, aren't I? Then you'll agree to our courtship, or do I have to 'speak to your guardian'?" he asked jokingly.

"I..." Blair began, but paused. Although his words had not been said with any intensity, his eyes told her just how serious he was being. "All right, Sean, we'll try again, but slowly this time."

"Good!" he declared. Then he lifted his arm, his hand open and waiting for hers to join with it. "Come with me."

When her hand was securely within his and the gentle warmth of their contact began to tingle along her arm, she spoke again. "Where are we going?"

"You'll see," was all that Sean would say.

And Blair did see. First they walked through the small streets and alleyways of old Charleston, looking into the small piazzas and gardens of the restored homes while they worked their way toward the center of the historical district. By the time they reached the more commercial area of old Charleston and started toward the docks it was past noon.

They ate lunch in a sidewalk café, sitting beneath an umbrella that kept the noonday sun at bay. During the meal of cold shrimp and salad, Sean surprised Blair for the second time when she asked how the reincarnation book was coming along.

"It's not," Sean said.

Blair shook her head reflexively. "What's wrong? Was it the research?" she asked.

"No," Sean said quickly as he reached across the table to cover her hand with his. "Did I ever tell you that my editor, Joyce—you remember, the blonde from the party," he added with a teasing smile. "She wanted me to do the reincarnation book as a novel?"

"No," Blair said. "Yes." She amended her answer when the memory of the conversation she'd overheard between Sean and Joyce at the cocktail party rose in her mind. "Yes, actually I overheard you and Joyce talking at the party. She said she thought it would be better as a novel."

"Good ears," Sean told her with a grin.

"Good memory," Blair replied pointedly.

"At any rate, when we were in Mexico, I began to get an idea for a novel using the reincarnation theme." Sean paused to look at Blair thoughtfully. "Sometimes when I get an idea, it takes so deep a hold on me that I have to write the story then. That's what happened with this idea."

"But the other book. Won't the publisher—"

"The publisher won't do a thing. They want novels from me. They were more than willing to extend the due date for the reincarnation book in favor of another Sean Mathias novel."

"I see," Blair whispered, feeling a degree of disappointment that the book she had worked so hard on was being postponed. But she shrugged the feeling away, knowing that Sean was too good a writer to do something that would hurt him or his career.

"What's the novel about?"

Sean smiled and slowly shook his head. "When it's finished, you'll know."

"That's not fair. First you tell me that you've changed direction in the middle of the river, and then you won't tell me where you're going to dock!"

"You know that writers are temperamental, don't you?"

"That's no excuse."

"I know," Sean said, his hand tightening on hers. "I write quickly. But this time, I surprised myself. In the four weeks since I started the novel, I've completed the first, very rough draft. I'm working on cleaning it up and fleshing it out. I think I'll have it done in another month or so.''

"So fast," Blair said, surprised.

"I had a lot of time alone to work on it. A lot of time," he reminded her pointedly.

"When can I read it?" she asked suddenly.

"Soon, I promise."

"All right," Blair said with a smile. "How 'bout a hint?"

"Hint?"

"About the novel."

"Waitress." Sean called, ignoring Blair's question as he waved over the waitress and asked for the check.

After they left the restaurant, they continued exploring the city. They went to the old market, which had been converted into a combination specialty boutique mart and a flea market.

From there, with their arms filled by a variety of items they'd purchased, they went to an ice cream parlor and sat, almost exhausted and devoured matching sundaes.

By six Blair could hardly walk and Sean hired a horse and carriage. The ride took fifteen minutes to reach the house on Church Street, where a tired Blair said goodbye until nine, when Sean said he would pick her up and take her to dinner.

At the large mahogany door, Blair looked up into his handsome face and smiled. "Thank you," she said simply.

"You're welcome," he replied, bending to kiss her lightly. Blair stayed at the door until he returned to the carriage and left. When the carriage turned the corner, Blair lingered for a few more moments to listen to the echo of the horse's hooves on the brick street. Slowly, with mixed feelings of weariness and contentment, she opened the door and went inside.

Blair lay in the large bathtub, letting her skin be warmed by the hot, relaxing water as she thought about the week that had just ended and the days that had flown by in a whirlwind of adventure and romance. Sean was treating her like a heroine from one of his novels; dining, dancing and waiting on her hand and foot. Each day starting at noon when Sean stopped work was filled with sightseeing, laughter and the pure enjoyment of being together.

Blair was quick to realize that this time their relationship was vastly different from what it had been before. They were taking the time to learn about each other, talking about their lives openly and about their goals for the future. Blair was no longer waiting for each day to end so she could find escape from reality in sleep.

In fact, Blair realized, she'd gotten to the point of dreading that time of night when Sean would return her to the house on Church Street, walk her to the front door and then chastely kiss her good-night before he disappeared into the darkness, whistling one silly tune or another.

Resting her head on the porcelain edge of the claw-foot bathtub, Blair felt her eyes begin to close and willed them to stay open. Tonight was to be a special night. Yesterday she had realized that she no longer felt the need to hide from the world, and had told Sean so. She'd also told him that she had decided to go back to New York and back to work.

He had greeted her words with a mixture of disappointment and approval. Disappointment, he'd said, because their romantic fantasy would soon be over. Approval, he'd added, because now their lives could once again start moving forward.

Blair had made a reservation for her return flight to New York for tomorrow evening. Sean would be on the same flight.

Earlier that day, while she and Sean had been out walking, she had impulsively bought an expensive new evening dress. They had been in the old section of town when she'd seen the dress hanging seductively in a shop window.

Without stopping to think about what she was doing, Blair had gone inside with Sean in tow, and made him wait while she tried it on. When she'd looked critically at herself in the dressing-room mirror, the salesgirl had echoed her own thoughts.

"You look beautiful in the dress," she'd said. And Blair had seen that she did, indeed look beautiful in the shimmering silk. She looked more sensual than she had in any other dress she'd ever worn before.

"But you can't wear a bra with it," the salesgirl had said, pointing to the lines of the bra material that showed through the fabric of the dress.

After she'd looked at herself for another minute, Blair decided to buy the dress. However she had not left the dressing room to show Sean the dress; instead, she'd asked the salesgirl if the dress could be delivered to her that afternoon so she could wear it that night.

When they emerged from the dressing room, Blair had taken out her charge card. Just as she'd handed the card to the salesgirl, Sean had gently stopped her. There had been several large bills in his hand.

"No," Blair had told him, "I pay for my own things."

Sean had shrugged then, but Blair had felt a distinct coolness come between them for a little while after they'd left the shop. A block later Blair had stopped to talk to him.

"Why is it bothering you that I wanted to pay for the dress myself?"

Sean had gazed at her for a moment and then looked past her. "Because I like buying you presents. And because I dislike being argued with."

"I didn't argue with you. I just didn't accept your money."

"Why, Blair? Were you afraid to? Were you afraid that it meant a commitment on your part if I paid for the dress?"

"I wasn't..." she had begun to say, a quick denial in her mind. But a moment later, she'd shaken her head. "Perhaps I was, Sean. I'm not sure. All I know is that I won't be bought."

"I'm not trying to buy you, Blair, only to make you happy."

As she'd stared at him, she'd believed his words. "That's all I want to be, Sean. Can we forget what happened?"

"Of course we can," he'd responded, warmth again emanating from him. The rest of the afternoon had passed pleasantly and Blair had been able to push the memory of that short, unpleasant time away.

But I will not be bought, she repeated silently to herself. *I am my own person.* Then Blair sat up in the tub and began to wash herself with the fragrant floral soap she had bought a few days before.

Fifteen minutes later she stepped from the tub and dried herself. After wrapping the towel around her, she went into the bedroom and sat at the white dressing table. Staring into the mirror, Blair took stock of herself.

Her face was deeply tanned after spending a week beneath the strong South Carolina sun, and she deemed that only a little makeup would be needed. While she primped her damp curls into the style she wanted and started to apply her eye shadow, Blair thought of the evening ahead.

Sean had told her that tonight he would be taking her to a special restaurant, one that would make her last night in Charleston outshine all the others. With a subdued thrill of excitement, she wondered what kind of a place he'd found—she had thought that they'd exhausted all the eating spots in Charleston.

Sighing, Blair finished her makeup and looked at herself again. The emerald green eye shadow emphasized the color of her eyes, while the smoothly applied mascara made them look large and bold. The finishing touch was the plum colored lipstick she applied with a small brush.

Leaving the dressing table, Blair crossed the room and began to dress. After putting on her panties and half-slip, she reached for the dress she'd bought that afternoon. The green silk almost matched the color of her eye shadow and when she'd slipped the dress on, the silk felt wonderfully cool against her skin.

Walking slowly to the full-length mirror set in a white lacquered frame, Blair was overly conscious of the way the silk rubbed her breasts and suddenly felt a little uncomfortable about not wearing a bra. However, when she saw her reflection gazing back at her so approvingly from within the mirror's depths, her discomfort quickly departed.

The dress looked perfect just the way it was, held up by thin spaghetti straps that connected at the top of the bodice and rose over each shoulder. The silk cupped her breasts gently, leaving very little to the imagination yet looking anything but vulgar. The dress narrowed at her waist, following the contours of her body before flaring gently outward to cover her hips, while at the same time flowing in a way that outlined the outside of her thighs.

Returning to the closet, Blair chose a pair of open-toed beige heels and slipped them on. As she finished putting few items into her clutch, there was a knock at the door.

"Yes?"

"Mr. Mathias is here," Mrs. Hadley said as she stepped into the white bedroom. Then she paused as she looked Blair over. "Now don't ya'll look just lovely. He's one lucky man," she added with a smile.

"He is, isn't he?" Blair returned with a light laugh.

"A handsome one too," the older woman added. "Wait till you see him. Oh, he's in the salon, I made him a drink."

"Thank you, Mrs. Hadley. I'm going to miss you," she said suddenly.

"We've loved having you here," the older woman said with a bright smile.

"I've really enjoyed myself. Thank you."

Mrs. Hadley nodded. "If you'll tell me what you'll be wearing tomorrow, I'll get the rest of your things packed tonight."

"That won't be necessary. I'll take care of it myself," Blair said. Picking up her clutch, she smiled at the older woman and started from the room. Blair paused in the hallway at the head of the stairs. A strange feeling came over her, and she gripped the banister tightly.

What's wrong? An instant later, she knew. As it had happened that night in Mexico City, over a month before, she knew that once again her life was about to change. *I will not be hurt by him again,* she told herself adamantly.

Chapter Twelve

Blair went through the doors that separated the main hallway from the salon. Once inside, she stopped, transfixed by what she saw. Sean was standing in two-thirds profile, looking out the large bay windows. The sight of his sleek physique combined with his formal clothing took her breath away.

A superbly fitting white evening jacket covered his broad shoulders and showed the full breadth of his back. She could just make out the black-studded formal dress shirt that was topped with a black silk hand-knotted formal bow tie. The gleaming black pants encasing his powerful legs were the perfect counterpoint to the white dinner jacket. His patrician face looked more than just handsome as he studied whatever it was he was looking at. His hand, tanned bronze from the sun, held a glass. His whole attitude was a study in confidence.

"You look like a dream come true," Sean said an instant before he turned to face Blair.

"I almost forgot your predilection for watching people's reflections in windows," Blair replied with a smile as the memory of that long ago night surfaced in her thoughts.

"Thank you for the compliment," she added as she closed the distance between them. "And you, sir, are beautiful."

"Beautiful?" Sean asked with upraised eyebrows.

Blair nodded. "Beautiful."

"In that case, thank you. I feel honored."

"Do you like the dress?" Blair asked, pirouetting before him.

"I like what's inside much better," he answered as his eyes devoured her. "And yes, I like the dress very much."

"Again, thank you," she said with a slight curtsy, playing the game out to its fullest. "Are you ready?"

Sean put his glass on the table and stepped closer. Taking her into his arms, he kissed her deeply.

Blair responded immediately to the kiss and could not help but enjoy the feel of her breasts being crushed against the hardness of his muscular chest. The kiss seemed to last forever, until Blair's legs wobbled uncertainly.

"I'm always ready for you," he said in a husky voice, when he released her.

Blair was conscious of the heavy rise and fall of his chest and the boldly open look of desire written upon his features.

"Ready for dinner.... No! Don't say it," she cried with a half laugh as her fingers flew to seal his lips. He kissed her fingers and then put his hands on her slim waist and drew her to him. The warmth of his breath on her cheek sent a shock wave of excitement through her.

"I love the way you feel against me," he murmured softly before releasing her.

Blair smiled, not betraying how shaken she was as she took his arm and then walked from the room. Outside, Blair's breath caught again when she saw that he had a horse and carriage waiting for them.

"Again?" she asked, pleased that he'd thought to do this.

"Anything for you, my New York southern belle," he told her as he helped her into the carriage.

The night was moonless; the black velvet of the sky was broken only by the glittering sequins of the stars that peeped from behind the clouds. With Blair's head resting on his shoulder, Sean let his mind roam. He fully enjoyed their closeness and cared little about when the ride would end. But the trip passed quickly as the warm night air, lacking the heavier humidity of the daytime, caressed them.

The carriage rolled slowly along Bay Street, the hoofbeats of the horse mingling pleasantly with the present-day sounds that were always nearby. The blocks slipped by until the carriage turned at Charlotte Street, and Blair thought absently that she'd not been on this street before.

"Where are we going?" she asked Sean in a throaty whisper. His hand caressed her shoulder; heat blazed upon her skin.

Instead of answering her, he raised his arm and pointed toward a replica of an old ship and then to the sign above it.

"My goodness," she whispered. "Really?"

"Really," Sean replied.

Blair stared wide-eyed as she descended from the carriage and then walked up the boarding plank of the ship. It was a floating restaurant done in antebellum style. The people working on the ship were dressed in the clothing of the bygone era of the 1850s, and they all acted their parts to the hilt.

She and Sean were led to a table in the main dining room, where a band played music from those gone, but apparently not forgotten, days. They dined on food that Blair had only read about, and attempted to dance the dances she had seen performed in old costume melodramas. She almost felt as though she were a heroine out of the pages of a romantic historical or an actress playing the lead in a movie. All she was lacking was an antique gown; she already had her hero with her.

All through dinner the electric tension enveloping them continued to grow. Every accidental touch of their fingers released sparks of lightning within her body. And for the first time since arriving in Charleston, Blair gave herself over to the feelings and emotions that swelled within her heart.

When dinner was over, Sean took Blair on a tour of the old ship. They went up to the bridge to look out at the Cooper River. Across the wide body of water, the lights of civilization flickered. But for all Blair cared they could have been lights from another world.

Then Blair went to the large wheel and grasping two of the spindle handholds, she pretended that she was the captain of the ship, steering it toward a new destination. Sean stood close behind her, and she sensed the smile that had to be on his face.

"Time to go, captain," she heard Sean whisper. Blair froze. She didn't want this night to end; she wanted it to go on for all eternity.

Turning, Blair gazed at him and saw that she had been wrong. Sean was not smiling; rather, his face was set in hard, serious lines. His hand rose to caress her face. Impulsively, Blair grasped his hand and moved it to her lips, holding his warm palm against her mouth and letting her lips drink in the special flavor of his skin. She knew that for them the evening might be ending, but it was the future that was just beginning.

They stayed like that for several long moments, until Sean gently withdrew his hand. When he offered her his arm, she slipped hers through it, and arm in arm they descended onto the main deck and then went down the boarding ramp and onto the street without speaking one word.

The same carriage they had arrived in was waiting for them, and Sean gallantly helped her into it. The return ride to Church Street was made in a deepening silence. Sean's arm was about her shoulders once more, holding her securely to him. Neither wanted to speak, for if they did, they would have to admit that the wonderful week they'd spent together was at an end.

When the carriage approached the large white house, Sean turned slightly, drawing Blair into a close embrace. She gazed up into his face and knew that he was going to kiss her parted lips. Like a movie shown in slow motion, his lips came to hers. She heard a throaty growl come from him, and the liquid fire within her erupted as their tongues met.

All too soon, Blair realized that the carriage had stopped. Sean released her slowly and stepped down. After he had helped her down, he paid the driver. Then he turned to Blair.

"I'm not leaving you, not yet. I want to stay for a while," he told her, his eyes locking with hers.

Under his unyielding stare, Blair's voice fled. She could only nod, knowing that she could no longer fight his needs or her own.

Together, and once again in silence, they climbed the steps to the front door, entered the house and then Blair led Sean up the wide staircase and into her room. Inside, Blair paused in surprise at the way the room shimmered with soft light.

Looking around, Blair saw that all the wall sconces had been lit and were illuminating the room with a dreamlike glow. On the small table by the double window sat a decanter of brandy and two snifters. Blair felt a rush of warmth for Mrs. Hadley. It was as if Mrs. Hadley had known more about Blair than she did herself.

"This room is magnificent," Sean said in an awed tone. "He recreated the past."

"No, he just brought it back," Blair corrected as she went to the small table. "Brandy?" she asked, gazing intently at Sean.

Sean nodded and started toward her, but stopped after only a few steps. He looked around the room once more and then shook his head. "And I thought

I was being so masterful when I said I wasn't leaving you tonight. I guess we both felt the same things about tonight and each other."

Blair paused, the crystal decanter wavering aloft as she looked at him. "Not quite," she replied. "I didn't plan this. In fact, I had no idea you'd be here with me tonight. No, this was Mrs. Hadley's handiwork, not mine."

Then Blair turned to finish pouring the amber liquid into the crystal snifters as Sean came up to her. His hands went around her waist to gently caress her stomach. His fingers, on the silk dress, sent rippling shivers along the surface of her skin.

Turning slowly, Blair presented him with his snifter. Silently, they both inhaled the heady fragrance of the brandy before taking a sip. "Blair," Sean began.

Suddenly Blair knew what she wanted and what she did not want for her life. And she wanted Sean to be a part, a very important part of her life. "Shhh..." she ordered.

Lifting onto the balls of her feet, she reached toward his mouth. When they kissed, it was like a butterfly skipping across her lips, but just the same, her breath exploded outward.

"You are the most beautiful creature I've ever known."

"And you've known many," Blair said before she could stop herself. "I'm sorry," she apologized, stepping back to take his free hand in hers. "I really am."

Sean stared down at her for a moment. The anger that had risen at her words dissipated when he read the truth within her eyes. And then his desire for her grew even stronger than it had been. Sean put his snifter down, the brandy still untasted. He took Blair's glass and placed it next to his. His hand tightened on hers as he drew her toward him.

The heat flaring from both of them was so intense that Blair thought she would melt when her body touched his and she leaned against him. Later, she could not remember who had undressed whom. All she knew was that their bare bodies had come together on the soft feathered mattress of the four-poster bed in a dance of passion that had almost robbed her of all her senses.

But even as their passion broke free and tried to overrule their hearts and minds, their love rose to give them back their reason. Their bodies slowed and they reacquainted themselves with each other in a more tender way.

"I've missed you more than I could ever put into words," Sean whispered when they had both gotten their runaway emotions under control.

"I...I've missed you too," Blair confessed as one lonely tear escaped her eye.

"I love you, Blair," Sean stated.

Their mouths came together then in a kiss that deepened, but did not erupt with uncontrollable passion. And after Blair drew her lips from his, she rested her head at the joining of his neck and shoulder. Her hand moved in lazy circles on his flat stomach for a little while until it started upward. She could feel each individual hair her fingertips floated over, and her feeling of love and warmth grew stronger.

Sean lay still, his breathing deep, his heart beating powerfully while his hand caressed the smoothness of Blair's back. With his desires in control, he marveled at the way he and Blair were in this moment in time, and was content just to lie with her and hold her close.

A few moments later Blair moved her head to better drink in the heady scent of Sean's body. She ran her lips across his chest kissing and tasting his taut skin.

His hand grew more insistent upon her, and she once again felt that funny, rippling sensation that always accompanied his touch. She tasted his hard, tight nipples for endless moments until she finally allowed her passion and desire to take control of her actions. Blair pressed herself along the length of his body, feeling every inch of his powerful strength. Then suddenly Sean's hands wound into her hair and drew her mouth to his, while at the same time he rolled them over in the bed. Then, like a Greek statue come to life within the flickering candles of the bedroom, he rose over her and plunged deeply within her.

Fire burned through her veins. She felt his heated length within her and trembled with need in his hard, masculine embrace. The hair on his chest rubbed against her breasts with a sensuality she thought she would be unable to endure for much longer.

And then Blair's mind lost its mooring within her body and she began to rise above everything, carried aloft by their strength and love. The passions he evoked within her brought every part of her alive, and soon her body exploded, and the luxurious comfort of Sean's body was again pressing down upon her. She held him tightly, her arms locked around his back, and lingeringly kissed his cheek.

She was content once again and complete, she believed, as as she lay securely in the afterglow of their lovemaking. A little while later, still held securely within his arms and bathed by his warmth, Blair fell into a deep and peaceful sleep.

Blair's last day in Charleston started differently from all the ones before it. When she awoke, the sun was not streaming through the white gauze curtains as it had every morning for the past week. Opening her eyes slowly, Blair turned to look at Sean.

He was gone. But no fear rose within her mind. She instinctively knew that he had gone back to the hotel to work. Although she was lonely waking without him, she also felt more alive this morning than she had since that terrible night in Mexico City.

Rising slowly, Blair readied her mind for her final day of vacation. She went to the window as she had each morning and looked out at the harbor. Gray clouds filled the sky, blotting out the sun and giving the day an overcast, almost ominous, appearance. But today Blair did not care. She was happy and in love.

After showering, Blair picked out a pale sundress, which would be comfortably cool in today's humidity and also be suitable for the flight home. She liked the looseness of the dress and knew the color looked good on her. Slipping into her sandals, Blair started out of the bedroom, but stopped. Her hands went to her ears and she realized that she had not put on her earrings. A brief moment later, with two oblong golden earrings in her lobes, Blair left the bedroom and went downstairs.

Before going into the kitchen, she decided to call Sean. When she heard his voice on the phone, a pleasantly warm sensation stole over her.

"Working hard?" she asked.

"Only until twelve," he replied.

"Shall I pick you up or meet you?" Blair asked.

"I'll meet you at...remember the sidewalk café we had lunch at the first day?" he asked.

"Uh-huh, at noon?"

"Noon," Sean agreed.

"Sean, I love you," she whispered just before she replaced the receiver in its cradle.

Then Blair went through the kitchen and out to the piazza, where she ate a freshly baked corn muffin with strawberry jam and then drank two cups of chicory-laced coffee.

After thanking Mrs. Hadley for a wonderful breakfast, Blair returned to her room and began packing. Once all her things were neatly packed in her two suitcases, she looked around the room to make sure she hadn't forgotten anything.

When she was satisfied that she'd left nothing behind, she glanced at her watch and saw that it was only ten-thirty. She still had an hour and a half before meeting Sean. With nothing else to do, she decided to take a walk through the enchantingly narrow streets and to look, for one last time, at the houses that had been resurrected from the past.

Sean stood and stretched, trying to clear away the mists that the reading and rereading had covered his eyes with. Exhaling, Sean nodded to himself, satisfied with what he'd accomplished this week with his work.

He had gone over the first draft of his reincarnation novel, making whatever changes he felt were necessary and putting in notes for parts he wanted fleshed out more fully.

As far as he was concerned, the manuscript was a good one, and he was sure that his editor would be satisfied. *But first I want Blair to read it,* he decided. Sean was happy with the way things had turned out between him and Blair and knew that this time their love would not fall apart or be threatened by misunderstandings. Yet he still felt a sense of wrong, knowing that he had not yet told Blair the full truth about the Mexican incident.

I will when we're in New York, he promised himself. Sean was positive that once he had told her what had really happened, and she had read the novel, she would understand everything. He believed that their love would not permit her to get so angry she would not be able to understand.

Sean smiled at his thoughts just as the phone rang. He reached for the receiver and spoke as he lifted it. "Hello?"

"Hi, Sean, how are you?" Alice Daniels asked.

"You couldn't wait until we got back to find out what happened, could you?"

"I figured that you and Blair had mended your fences, since I didn't hear from either of you," Alice stated calmly.

"Yes, we did mend our fences. And you've been selling too many westerns," he added jokingly.

"I haven't sold one in three years. But I did sell a few true confessions," Alice joked. Then her voice turned serious again. "I told you that Blair would believe the truth if you told it to her," Alice stated confidently. "I was right, wasn't I?"

Sean took a deep breath before he replied. "Ah...Alice, I wasn't exactly able to do that."

"You what!" Alice exploded. "You promised me that if I told you where she was, you would tell her the truth!"

"I tried Alice, but she wouldn't listen. But I didn't lie, not really."

"What else could you do if you didn't lie?" Alice charged.

"Not tell her anything. She was so mad at me that I just told her that I wouldn't explain. That she would have to take me on trust. What I told Blair was that I loved her and that Elaina was in the past."

"Oh, Sean, I'm getting a bad feeling. You should have told her," Alice said in a low voice.

"Told her what? Do you think that she would have believed me if I said that I was calling her by the name of a woman I created on paper? Would you?"

"I'm not Blair."

"I know. Alice...how could I tell her, as upset as she was, that I used her as the model for a woman who's been dead for two hundred years; and then I stupidly called Blair the dead woman's name because I was caught up in the story idea?" Sean paused for a moment to take a breath.

"Besides," he said after a brief pause, "when she reads the manuscript, she'll understand."

"I hope so. How is the rewrite coming along?"

"Good. Oh, there is one part I want your opinion on. Do you have a minute?"

"Go ahead."

Sean rifled through the typewritten pages until he came to one with several handwritten pages attached to it. After separating them, he began to speak again.

"This is the part where Matt—the man structured after Raul, Marylena's lover—finds Marylena's present-day incarnation. I didn't think it was strong enough, so I added a few things."

"'I've waited for two centuries to find you. And I don't care that your hair is short and your eyes are hazel and not blue. It doesn't matter that your name is not Elaina any more, because I'm not a stable boy in this lifetime! All that matters is that we be together again and fulfill the destiny that is ours and ours alone!'

"'You have to understand that we belong together. Always! And whatever lifetimes we've been apart and whatever loves we've experienced without each other can only make us love each other more.'"

Without realizing it, Sean's voice had risen as he read the dialogue he'd written. Suddenly the words he'd read Alice vanished from his thoughts as another, vastly more important, thought overrode them. "Alice," he asked in a slightly lower voice, "do you think that Blair will understand?"

"I hope so," Alice replied. "By the way, that was quite good."

"Thanks. I'll talk to you tomorrow."

"Good luck, Sean."

Sean hung up the phone and looked at his watch. It was ten to twelve. In ten minutes he would be with Blair. Thinking about her made him think about Alice's words.

I'll tell her as soon as we get back to New York, he promised himself again.

By eleven-thirty, Blair had done all the sightseeing she wanted to and tried to think of a way to kill the half hour. Acting on impulse, she decided not to meet Sean at the restaurant; rather, she would surprise him and pick him up at the hotel.

She took her time walking to the hotel, not wanting to disturb Sean while he was working. But ten minutes later she reasoned that he would have to stop soon so that he could get ready for their date.

At a quarter to twelve, Blair entered the air-conditioned lobby of the elegant hotel and went to the house phones. She dialed Sean's room and got a busy signal for her efforts.

Shrugging, Blair hung up the phone and went to the bank of elevators, deciding to go upstairs and collect him personally. The ride to the third floor seemed endless, but eventually she reached Sean's room.

A thrill of anticipation at seeing the surprised look on his face filled her as she lifted her hand to knock. Before her hand reached the wood, she heard the distinct sound of his voice through the closed door.

"I've waited for two centuries..."

Blair stood, frozen to the spot as Sean's words battered at her mind. She wanted to turn and run but refused to give in to that weakness. She remembered the times she had run from him and the pain she'd felt when she had. This time she had to wait and find out what was happening. Slowly, she lowered her hand and continued to listen.

"We belong together. Always! Whatever lifetimes we've had apart and whatever loves we've experienced without each other can only make us love each other more."

Again Blair's mind spun madly, her thoughts became mired in the fog that was fast consuming her head. Blinking several times, Blair once again tried to understand what was happening. *Who was Sean talking to?*

But even as she tried to puzzle out the answers, she heard Sean speak again.

"Alice," her numbed ears heard him say, "do you think that Blair will understand?"

Blair's hand flew to her mouth. "No!" she cried into her trembling fingers, shaking her head at the same time. Her mind whirled and the light began to dim before her, blotting out all the joy and happiness of moments before.

Then Blair could listen no longer. Her ears refused to hear and her mind would not accept what she'd already heard. Her world was once again irrevocably shattered. Holding back a sob, Blair fled the hotel.

When she finally stopped walking and was able to make her mind function again, she discovered that she was on Bay Street.

Pictures of the past days paraded before her eyes. She and Sean on their shopping expeditions, the open-air lunches and romantic dinners and the hours spent talking and learning to trust again. The trips to the various plantations and gardens surrounding Charleston were vividly replayed before her eyes. A picnic amidst the splendor and grandeur of the Magnolia Gardens flashed up before her.

Sitting on a bench under a tree, Blair closed her eyes. Gone was the feeling of contentment. It had been replaced by an emotional dirge that dragged at her heart.

How could I believe him, she asked herself when she was able to think about what he'd said. Although she hadn't wanted to think about what had happened, she knew she had no choice. His words evoked too much pain to ignore. And as she replayed what Sean had said to Alice, she began to despise herself for loving him.

The more she thought about what Sean had said, the more certain she was about its meaning. She believed Sean thought her to be the reincarnation of a former love. And worse, everything he'd said pointed to his belief that she was the reincarnation of Marylena Montez. *Impossible!*

Suddenly, Blair felt a strange calmness descend upon her, allowing her to think clearly. All the facts she had discovered in Mexico came to mind. That Marylena Montez had been dead for two centuries; that she had had long hair and blue eyes. And that she had taken on the name of Elaina.

What had he said, she asked herself. "I don't care that her hair is short and her eyes are hazel and not blue." *My hair is short. My eyes are hazel.*

She also remembered, from their time in Mexico, asking Sean who the man was who believed he was Marylena Montez's reincarnated lover, Raul.

"A man with ambitions and desires like any other," Sean had told her.

"Liar!" she whispered. *It wasn't just any man. Sean was Raul!* There could be no other explanation. *And he thinks that I'm Marylena Montez.*

In that moment, with the understanding of everything she valued in life growing strong within her heart and mind, Blair knew she was facing a decision that would affect all her remaining years.

Standing, Blair crossed the street and went to the edge of the water. She looked into the murky depths and brought forth the possibility of never seeing Sean again; of never feeling his strong and gentle hands upon her skin; of never hearing his deep laughter or seeing the passion pour from his eyes while he gazed at her.

"I can't give him up again," she whispered to the choppy water.

Wiping the tears that traced their way down her cheeks, and with the full acceptance that she was damning herself to a life that would always be shadowed with sorrow, Blair made the only decision she could. She had found love again after too many years, and she would not—she could not—give that love up. She would fight, she would make him desire only her and not some ghost of the past that he believed her to be. She would teach him to love her and only her, not the dead woman he mistakenly believed she had been in some past lifetime.

With her mind made up and her heart bolstered, with her new resolve firmly in place, Blair left to meet Sean.

When she arrived at the restaurant, Sean was already there, seated at a table next to the railing, sipping from a glass of sparkling water. His shirt collar was open just enough to reveal a glimpse of the dark hair on his chest, and with an apprehensive intake of breath, Blair joined him.

As she sat, the radiance of his smile did little to add to her confidence. Her appetitie had deserted her earlier, and it had not returned. She sensed that Sean was able to tell that something was bothering her.

When the waitress came to take their order, Blair looked up. "I'm not ready yet," she said. The waitress left quickly.

"What's wrong?" Sean asked, his gaze piercing into her heart.

Blair shook her head; she wasn't ready to trust her tongue yet.

"Do you want to talk about it?" Sean persisted, gazing steadily at her. He knew something was bothering her, but he wasn't sure what it was.

Then he smiled. He remembered all too well her feelings about commitment and knew that throughout the beautiful night they'd shared he had not once mentioned the future.

Slowly, with his smile growing, he reached into his pants pocket and grasped the emerald ring. "Blair, I've told you many times that I loved you. It seems that I've always loved you. It's hard to explain, but when I'm with you, I feel as though we've always been together and that we always will be, no matter what."

Pausing, Sean brought his hand up to the table. When the back of his hand was resting in the exact center of the white tablecloth, he opened his fist to show her the ring resting in his palm.

"I gave this to you once, and you gave it back to me. Take it, Blair."

Blair stared at the ring, her mind once again threatening to shut down. All her hard-earned resolve fell away, and the promises she'd made to herself were broken before she could even try.

The words he had just spoken were the all-too-present proof of the impossibility of what she wanted. They confirmed just how much he believed she was who he wanted her to be.

Slowly, with her head shaking in sorrow, she pushed herself from the table and stood. When she spoke, her voice was as cold as an Arctic wind. "I can't be who you want me to be! Nor is love something that can be created out of the ashes of the past. I am Blair Sanders, not some long dead woman. Go find your Elaina—your Marylena—in another lifetime, not in mine!"

With that, Blair turned and walked away.

Chapter Thirteen

Sean stared at Blair's retreating back, his muscles as frozen as his mind, while he tried to digest what had just happened. Shaking his head slowly, he curled his fingers tightly over the emerald ring, securing it within his fist.

Nothing she'd said to him made any sense. *What in the hell did Marylena Montez have to do with us?* Then Sean became angry. With everyting he had tried to do and at every point where he'd tried to show her how much he loved her, she had turned what he did into something different.

No more! She won't do this to me again, Sean told himself. *That is the last time I'll play her pointless game!* After returning the ring to his pocket, he took out a ten-dollar bill and dropped it on the table. Then he left the restaurant and returned to the hotel.

In his room, his anger still unabated, he called the airport to change his return flight to New York. He didn't even want to be on the same plane with her. After getting confirmation for a first-class seat on the last fight of the day, Sean picked up the manuscript he'd been working on and started to look it over again.

He'd stared at the page but did not see any of the words typed upon it. All he saw was Blair's face, the outrage plainly visible on it.

Closing his eyes, he forced the memory from before him and willed himself to concentrate. But again he could not get past the first word.

"Damn her!" he shouted at the pages.

A strange lethargy had captured Blair by the time she reached the house on Church Street, but she did not allow that or her unhappiness to show. The first thing she did was to call the airport to rearrange her flight. She did not want to take the same plane as Sean and had been able to get a business-class seat on the six o'clock flight without a problem. With several hours on her hands before she was due to leave for the airport, Blair left the house and went across the street to the park.

Sitting on a bench, she began to think about what her life might have been like if Sean had loved her and had not had this ridiculous obsession with a woman who had died over two hundred years before.

How could I have been so stupid, she asked herself. And then she thought about something that Sean had once said. "You have no choice about who you fall in love with." It was true, Blair realized, she'd had no choice when she'd fallen in love with him. She had tried not to love him, she had tried and failed.

Blair gazed up at the cloud-filled sky. *What do I do now? He's been in my blood since I first met him. He's in my heart.*

Why couldn't I pretend? Why wasn't I able to hold back my anger and make him love me for myself? But Blair knew the answer to that question. She didn't want to *make* him love her, she needed his freely given love, not the love he had for another person.

While Blair's mind continued to roam wildly, her hand absently rose to worry her left earlobe. An instant after touching her earlobe, her myriad thoughts vanished. The earring was gone. She checked her right ear and found the other earring securely in place. She looked at the bench and then at the ground, but realized that she could have lost it anywhere.

"Today must be my day to lose things," she whispered as she thought of the earrings she'd worn almost every day during her stay in Charleston—the earrings that had been her favorites for almost a year. Slowly, she took out the remaining oblong golden earring and put it into her purse.

Blair sat in the park for three more hours, her mind lodged within a dark haze of tortured thoughts. The future, which had seemed so bright when she'd awakened this morning, now appeared to be an unfathomable mist-shrouded mystery. And Blair knew that she had indeed lost a deep love for the second time in her life.

After shoring up her badly shaken mind, Blair willed strength into her limbs and left the park. The first thing she saw when she entered the large white house was her luggage. Looking at the antique grand-father clock in the hallway, she saw that it was almost four and that it was time to call a taxi.

Before she could do that, the Hadleys appeared from out of the kitchen. "I was just going to bring the car around and load your luggage," Mr. Hadley explained, pointing to the two suitcases.

"Thank you," Blair said with a smile of genuine warmth, her first since overhearing Sean's damning words. "But I don't want to put you to any trouble. I'll call a cab."

"Nonsense!" Clair Hadley stated. "Ya'll will most certainly allow Charles to drive you to the airport. Why, Mr. Marks would never forgive us if we didn't. Charles," she said pointedly.

"Thank you," Blair said as Charles Hadley left to get the car.

Mrs. Hadley smiled at Blair. "I do hope that the next time you're in these parts, you'll stop by and say hello. We've really enjoyed having someone in the house, especially when that someone is as nice as you. It gets lonely with only Charles," she said with a conspiratorial wink.

A moment later Mr. Hadley returned to get the suitcases and Blair. A half hour after that, Blair was at the ticket counter, exchanging her ticket on the earlier flight for the new one. With an hour to kill before her flight was to be called, Blair went into the cocktail lounge and sat in one of its dark corners.

By four o'clock, Sean could no longer stand the confines of his hotel room. He'd never got past the single page of the manuscript and between his inability to see the words he'd written and his angered and frustrated pacing, he knew he'd be better off waiting at the airport than hiding in his room.

And for more times than he wanted to think about over the past few hours, Sean had done his best to make himself try to forget Blair Sanders. He had also worked hard to convince himself that she no longer mattered to him. He had failed in both matters, utterly.

Pushing Blair momentarily from his thoughts, he called the front desk for a bellhop and then put his manuscript into his attaché case. A moment later Sean opened the door and stepped out of the room. Just as he reached the elevator, a glint of light caught his eye. Bending, Sean saw a small gold earring caught in the carpet.

Even as he reached for it, he recognized its oblong shape and was sure that it was one of the earrings that Blair had worn during their daily excursions over the past week.

Why is it here, he wondered. Once again, nothing that had happened today made any sense.

But by the time the elevator reached his floor and he began his final descent to the lobby, Sean had put together the random pieces of the puzzle. He understood why she had reacted the way she had at the outdoor café and why she had said those illogical things to him about Marylena Montez.

He was even able to figure out exactly what she'd overheard through the thin hotel-room door: it had been his conversation with Alice, and more than likely the few paragraphs he'd read aloud. Sean knew that Blair had either misunderstood what he was saying to

Alice or she had reacted to the knowledge that he had not told her the complete truth that first day in Charleston.

When Sean stepped out of the elevator, his face was no longer lined with tension. A half smile had replaced the tautness of his mouth while he had studied the earring. His determination to forget Blair started to diminish even as he began to think that there might be another chance for them.

Then another thought reared upward in his head. *Do I want to take that chance one more time?* Sean lifted the earring to study it. And, strangely, he did not know whether he wanted to take that chance or not. The smile left his face and tense lines returned to shadow his features.

But when he passed the counter of house phones, he stopped. She had been booked on the four o'clock flight. Glancing at his watch, he realized that the plane should have just taken off.

In case it was delayed, Sean called the house where Blair had been staying. When Mrs. Hadley answered, Sean asked if Blair had left.

"Just this minute, Mr. Mathias," she told him.

"Then her flight was delayed?" he asked.

"No, she changed to a later flight. The six o'clock plane."

"Thank you, Mrs. Hadley," Sean said as he lowered the receiver. Then he smiled. Apparently fate had conspired to make up his mind for him. And just maybe, he thought, something good might yet come out of this day.

Ten minutes after Sean paid his bill, he was in a taxi and on his way to the airport. The closer the cab got to the airport, the more determined Sean became to face Blair and make her see how foolish everything that had happened between them had been.

Suddenly Sean knew that he could not let her go and knew, too, that he would never have been able to do that.

Sitting at the airport lounge, Blair watched the multitude of people moving about, some purposefully, others aimlessly; both types reminded her of herself.

Ever since leaving the restaurant earlier that day, she had been moving purposely along a path she'd had no choice but to take; yet while she went about leaving Charleston, her mind wandered aimlessly whenever she lowered her guard.

Tears threatened to spill from her eyes, and Blair willed them away. Her hands grasped the table, and her knuckles turned white. She stared at the glass of club soda she had ordered but had not touched.

Why was I such a fool. Why did I believe he loved me? Blair knew there were no answers for her now, just as there had been none all day long.

Glancing at the clock on the far wall, Blair saw that it was almost five-thirty, and her flight would be called momentarily. She stood and left the lounge. As she stepped into the main flow of people, she looked up at the gate signs and then walked toward her departure gate and to the plane that would take her home. Suddenly Blair wanted nothing more than to be home and in familiar surroundings.

When she was almost at her gate, Blair froze. Leaning against a railing outside the waiting area and staring at her from beneath half-hooded eyes, was Sean. Her heart thudded loudly at the sight even as her mind screamed out its warning.

In an ethereal moment where time slowed and her senses were heightened, she watched Sean straighten and come toward her. His indolent smile was firmly fixed as he stepped in front of her and barred her from continuing on.

"Go away!" she whispered fiercely, but he continued to block her way.

"We have to talk," Sean stated.

"Not any more," Blair retorted quickly.

"You can either talk to me here or on the plane. I think here would be better. It will cause less of a scene."

"If you don't get out of my way, I'll show you exactly what causing a scene is all about," she snapped, her voice rising as she spoke. "I mean it!" she said, her voice loud in the long hall.

Unbelievably she saw Sean smile boldly. "Go ahead. Yell, shout, scream. When you're finished, we'll talk."

Blair sighed, but she was not willing to accept defeat so easily. "Sean," she began as she took a deep breath. "Get out of my way."

Sean shook his head and, ignoring the people who were now staring openly at them, reached for her. His hands tightened, vicelike on her arms and he drew her inexorably toward him. His eyes raked across her face, drinking in her angry but still beautiful features as he slowly lowered his mouth to hers.

Fighting against the loss of her love and against the rage that filled her at Sean's newest affront to her senses, Blair, in a last desperate effort, pulled free of his grip and stepped back.

"That's always your answer, isn't it?" she asked, not caring that her voice was raised and that her words were attracting everyone's attention. "Kiss me and try to make believe that you've done nothing wrong! That's your offense as well as your defense! But it won't work this time."

"What the hell is wrong with you!" Sean roared, his mind focused on only one thing. He did not see anyone else or care that they were attracting a crowd.

"What's wrong with me?" she asked, matching his roar with her own shout. "I'll tell you what's wrong with me. You are! You and your deceitfulness. Your lies are what's wrong with me!"

"I've never told you a lie!" he stated, his eyes never once leaving her face. His anger was growing out of proportion, and in a far corner of his mind he knew he had to regain some control over his emotions. But Blair's next words wiped away even that saving thought.

"You're lying to me right now! You've been lying to me ever since Mexico. Ever since you called me by *her* name."

Behind them, in the waiting area, they heard titters rising from the onlooker, but neither Sean nor Blair was willing to take their eyes from each other. Their faces were only inches apart. Sean stood above her, staring powerfully down while Blair matched his stare with her upturned face and thrusting chin.

"I tried to explain about Elaina. You wouldn't hear me out!"

"Hear you out when? That time in the park? That was no explanation," Blair stated, each word dripping venom. "You even had the blatant gall to use Brian's memory to placate me."

Sean fought to lower his voice, and won his small battle. "Are you done?" he asked in a lower voice.

"Not by a long shot!" Blair declared, unable to stop herself from venting all the hurt, anger, and above all, anguish that he had caused her. Behind Sean, she saw a woman smile at her and give her a thumbs-up, which she ignored completely.

"I believed what you told me," she stated. "And it was because I wanted to, because I loved you. I even let you make love to me again."

"Of course that was all one-sided, wasn't it. I remember how much you protested, how much you fought me when I *seduced* you!" he retorted sarcastically, his rage caused as much by the sound of her words as by their content.

"Damn you, Sean! I'm not some little tart you can play your games with, live out your strange fantasy with. I won't come jumping because you give me a bauble and profess eternal love," she stated, her voice changing from a high, shrill sound to a lower and more controlled volume.

When she finished, the loudspeaker announced that their flight was preparing to board, and the first section was asked to go to the gate. The crowd that had been watching them began to move away. Sean shook his head and reached toward her.

"Don't!" she ordered, stepping back. "I was at your hotel this morning. I was going to surprise you by picking you up for lunch. When I called your room, the line was busy, so I went upstairs." Blair paused to take a breath and to force herself to keep the small thread of control she had finally gained. "I heard you talking to Alice. You were speaking so loudly that I couldn't help but overhear."

Sean reached into his pocket and withdrew the earring. Holding his hand palm up, he looked into Blair's eyes. "I know," he told her in a husky whisper.

After staring at the golden oblong in his palm, Blair took a deep breath before shaking her head sadly. "It doesn't matter, does it? What I learned today when I overhead you hurt me deeply. But even then I tried to convince myself I could make you love me for myself and make you forget some woman you thought you loved in...in another lifetime. How could you do that to me?"

"You know," Sean began, his voice low, his tone thoughtful, "that you once said all we do is eat and argue. You were wrong. All we do is make love and then you run away from me."

"I think I've had reason enough," Blair stated as yet another section of passengers were called to board the plane.

"Perhaps you do believe you had sufficient reason to run away," Sean admitted.

But Blair wasn't sure whether it was an admission or just a statement of fact. Yet the pain that had seemed to flicker across his all-too-handsome face, made her think he was being honest, for the moment.

"I am sorry, Blair," he told her, his eyes again caressing her face.

"No! Don't look at me like that and don't be sorry! It's all for the best. You see," she said, refusing to meet his eyes fully, "after what happened today and after spending a lot of hours trying to understand what was so wrong with me that you had to love someone whom you think I once was, I realized that you would never see me for who I am. And, Sean, without that, we could never have a life together. I love you, but I can't be with you, knowing what I do."

And the tears she had been fighting ever since she'd fled the restaurant returned to wash silently down he cheeks. Yet the catharsis of her words was helping her to be strong enough to face what she knew she had to.

"You love me that much?" Sean asked in a voice that was caught with emotion. "Thank you," he said. Then he handed her the earring. "I do love you, Blair. Just you—no one else. I always have, but you haven't been able to see that. And I can't control the meanings that you put to the words you overheard me say. I can only tell you that you've made a mistake."

Pausing, Sean lifted his hand and gently wiped Blair's tears away. "This time I had hoped to make you listen instead of shutting me off. But I see now that that's impossible. Goodbye, Blair," he whispered.

Blair stood immobile as Sean walked to the small counter and handed the man at the desk his ticket. She did not move until Sean walked to the gate and disappeared from sight.

With a low sob that she almost held back, Blair repeated the process that Sean had just gone through. Five minutes later she was seated next to a window in the business class, which separated first class from coach. There she stared out the window, doing her best to ignore the people who tried to get a glance at the woman who had entertained them in the boarding area a short time before.

When the plane finally started to taxi, Blair sighed with relief. When the plane was airborne, things quickly changed again, as the stewardess came over to her and handed her a thick manila envelope.

"That's not mine," she told the woman.

"It has your name on it," the stewardess said, showing her that it was indeed her name written across the front. Unable to refuse the envelope, Blair took it and studied it.

"Now what?" she murmured, realizing almost too late that it was not a regular manila envelope but one that manuscripts were usually mailed in.

Opening the envelope, she withdrew a thick bundle of paper and stared at the first page and at Sean's name beneath the title.

Ashes of The Past was the handwritten title. Blair closed her eyes for a moment as the full impact of the words struck at her heart and mind. Then she looked at the next page and her eyes filmed with moisture. *This novel is dedicated with love to Blair Sanders, who helped me to discover Elaina and who eventually will discover Elaina for herself.*

"Damn you, Sean Mathias!" she whispered. When she looked at the third page, she saw that it was type-written, not handwritten, as were the first two. She also saw that it had been edited with a red marker. And as the plane banked in its final ascent before heading to New York, Blair gave up fighting and started to read.

For the two and a half hours of the flight and for the twenty minutes that the plane circled above a crowded

Kennedy Airport and even during the long twelve minutes that the plane taxied, Blair read Sean's manuscript.

When the plane stopped at the landing gate and the passengers were disembarking, Blair was on the last three pages. By the time she had finished the manuscript and dried her eyes once again, the plane was empty. She wished her mind were the same.

Moving as though she were in a fog, Blair put the manuscript back into the envelope and stood. She walked slowly to the exit and then nodded absently to the stewardesses, who thanked her for flying their airline.

She walked down the long ramp and then stepped into the arrival room. A moment later she saw Sean leaning against the railing. His face was set in serious lines and his eyes were almost expressionless.

Ever so slowly she walked toward him. When she was barely a foot away, she stopped and extended the manuscript to him.

"You're a bastard," she said.

Sean stared at her for a second before he exhaled slowly. "But at least I tried to make you see the truth. Goodbye," he said for the second time that day.

Before he was three steps away, Blair called out his name. Turning, he looked at her and waited.

"That's my title on your book."

"No, that was your statement," he corrected. "And titles cannot be copyrighted."

"Why did you dedicate it to me?"

"Because I love you. Because if it hadn't been for you, I would never have written the story."

"Damn it, Sean, why couldn't you tell me the truth?" she asked. She knew her eyes were pleading with him, but she could not hide the way she felt.

"I tried, Blair. I tried in New York and you kept hanging up on me. I tried again in Charleston and you put up a stone wall the instant I tried to speak the truth. I knew then that if I told you what had really happened, you would still think I was lying."

"What is the truth? Is the truth what you've written in that novel? Or is that just another fantasy you created?"

"Does it matter anymore?" he asked.

"It matters, Sean, it matters more than anything else."

Sean stared at her for another moment before his gaze softened. He took a single step toward her, then stopped again. "Trust and faith is what matters, Blair. Believing in your heart and your emotions matters."

"I'm trying to find a way to do that, Sean. But I can't do it without you. Help me, Sean, for the love that you say you have for me, help me."

Sean took a deep breath. "Elaina never existed except in my mind and on the pages of the manuscript you just read. I created her that last evening in Mexico at the same time that you were taking a shower. Do you remember when you came into my room and I was working?"

Blair nodded.

"I was putting down my ideas. I was creating a love scene between Elaina and Raul. The problem was that I used you—your features, your eyes, your hair and the way I see you—to create the character of Elaina.

"Blair, I'm a writer—a novelist. I have been since I was old enough to string words together. I can't separate my private personality from my writer's mind; they're one and the same. When I get an idea, it permeates my every thought until I have it down on paper and write The End at the bottom of the last page.

"When I kissed you that night and called you Elaina, it was because my idea for the novel was enmeshed within all my thoughts. And Blair, although Elaina was modeled after you, you're not Marylena Montez, nor did I ever think you were. And I am by no stretch of the imagination the reincarnation of Raul."

Through the confusing maze that his words had led her, Blair's thoughts emerged into the clarity of understanding. Her heart began to beat with more strength than it had since noon, but before she could say a word, Sean spoke again.

"If you've read the manuscript, then you've already learned that what you overheard was some of the rewritten dialogue that I was reading to Alice, who incidentally had spent ten minutes yelling at me for breaking my promise to her."

"Promise?"

"I made a deal with her. She told me where you ran away to—"

"I didn't run away!"

"And I promised that I would tell you the truth. It took awhile, but I finally managed to do just that. Or don't you believe me yet?"

Blair smiled a tight-lipped smile of acceptance that showed how hard she was battling to hold back her tears. "I..." but her emotions refused to let her speak.

She stared at Sean through mist-veiled eyes, and tried to speak again. "I love you, Sean. And I believe you."

The two steps that separated them vanished as they went into each others arms. Their mouths met in a kiss that echoed Blair's last words. Slowly the kiss deepened, and the fires of passion mixed with the gentle warmth of her love and Blair knew that the future was once again within her grasp.

When they parted, their hearts were beating as one. Silently, as Sean drew away, he put his arm about Blair's waist. She put her arm around his waist and they started toward the main terminal together.

When they were almost there, Blair spoke again, hesitantly. "When...when Dr. Eldridge hypnotized you, did you find a past life?" she asked.

Sean paused in midstride to stare down at her. An instant later he smiled. "Will you marry me?" he asked.

"Yes. Sean, about—"

"Children. We've never talked about children. Do you like them?"

"Sometimes. What happened with Dr. Eldridge?" she asked, unwilling to be put off again.

"Sometimes? That's honest enough. How many sometimes do you want?"

"Two. How many past lives have you had?"

"I love you," Sean stated.

"I love you, too. How many?"

"Children?"

"Sean!"

"The first time you asked me that, I told you that there has to be some mystery in love. I haven't changed my mind."

"And I'm a researcher. I have to find answers to my questions."

"Marry me tomorrow?" he asked.

"We need to wait for the blood tests," she said logically.

"We'll get them tomorrow."

"All right, Sean," she said in a low voice, her eyes caressing his face. "I won't push right now. And yes, I'll marry you as soon as we can be married."

"Thank you," he said, bending to brush his lips on hers. When he lifted his head again, he sighed. "Two."

"Lifetimes?" Blair asked, her shock evident in her voice.

"Children. I'd like two children," he told her.

"As long as they're not as insufferable as you!"

"All right," he said with a shrug.

Blair looked deeply into his eyes and what she saw there made her legs turn to rubber. "All right," she whispered. "But I won't give up trying to find the answer."

"I wouldn't love you if you did. Can we get your luggage now?"

"In a moment. There's one more matter I need to clear up."

Sean sighed again. "I thought we had everything settled," he told her, trying to figure out what he had forgotten.

"We're engaged now, correct?"

Sean nodded.

"Well?"

Sean stared at her, his face expressionless. Then he bent and kissed her. "Congratulations."

The laugh almost got away from her, but she caught it just in time and was able to keep a straight face. "That's not what I mean."

"What do you mean?"

"My ring," she whispered as she held up her hand and wiggled her ring finger.

She stared at him as he threw back his head and gave vent to his deep, wonderful laughter. When it ended, and he was looking at her again, she thought that her heart would burst with love.

"Forgive me," Sean said, reaching into his pocket to withdraw the ring once again. "I never did get a chance to put it back in its box," he whispered when he slipped the ring on her finger.

"Sean?" she called in a low voice as she raised her eyes from the ring and gazed deeply into his. "We're going to be very happy."

"Yes, we will be," he told her confidently. And then they were in each others arms again and they knew that they would be together for the rest of their lives.

READERS' COMMENTS ON SILHOUETTE SPECIAL EDITIONS:

"I just finished reading the first six Silhouette Special Edition Books and I had to take the opportunity to write you and tell you how much I enjoyed them. I enjoyed all the authors in this series. Best wishes on your Silhouette Special Editions line and many thanks."

—B.H.*, Jackson, OH

"The Special Editions are really special and I enjoyed them very much! I am looking forward to next month's books."

—R.M.W.*, Melbourne, FL

"I've just finished reading four of your first six Special Editions and I enjoyed them very much. I like the more sensual detail and longer stories. I will look forward each month to your new Special Editions."

—L.S.*, Visalia, CA

"Silhouette Special Editions are — 1.) Superb! 2.) Great! 3.) Delicious! 4.) Fantastic! . . . Did I leave anything out? These are books that an adult woman can read . . . I love them!"

—H.C.*, Monterey Park, CA

*names available on request

If you're ready for a more sensual, more provocative reading experience...

We'll send you
4 Silhouette Desire novels
FREE
and without obligation

Then, we'll send you six more Silhouette Desire® novels to preview every month for 15 days with absolutely no obligation!

When you decide to keep them, you pay just $1.95 each ($2.25 each in Canada) *with never any additional charges!*

And that's not all. You get FREE home delivery of all books as soon as they are published and a FREE subscription to the Silhouette Books Newsletter as long as you remain a member. Each issue is filled with news on upcoming titles, interviews with your favorite authors, even their favorite recipes.

Silhouette Desire novels are not for everyone. They are written especially for the woman who wants a more satisfying, more deeply involving reading experience. Silhouette Desire novels take you *beyond* the others.

If you're ready for that kind of experience, fill out and return the coupon today!

Silhouette ⭐ Desire®

Silhouette Books, 120 Brighton Rd., P.O. Box 5084, Clifton, NJ 07015-5084

**Clip and mail to: Silhouette Books,
120 Brighton Road, P.O. Box 5084, Clifton, NJ 07015-5084** *

YES. Please send me 4 FREE Silhouette Desire novels. Unless you hear from me after I receive them, send me 6 new Silhouette Desire novels to preview each month as soon as they are published. I understand you will bill me just $1.95 each, a total of $11.70 (in Canada, $2.25 each, a total of $13.50)—with no additional shipping, handling, or other charges of any kind. There is no minimum number of books that I must buy, and I can cancel at any time. The first 4 books are mine to keep.   **3D18R6**

Name	(please print)	
Address		Apt. #
City	State/Prov.	Zip/Postal Code

* In Canada, mail to: Silhouette Canadian Book Club, 320 Steelcase Rd., E.,
Markham, Ontario, L3R 2M1, Canada
Terms and prices subject to change.
SILHOUETTE DESIRE is a service mark and registered trademark.   **D-SUB-1**

Silhouette Special Edition

COMING NEXT MONTH

RETURN TO PARADISE—Jennifer West
Reeve Ferris was swiftly rising to stardom, yet he couldn't forget Jamie Quinn, the small-town girl who had captured his heart along the way.

REFLECTIONS OF YESTERDAY—Debbie Macomber
Angie knew the minute she saw Simon that twelve years had changed nothing; she was still destined to love him, and they still seemed destined to be kept apart.

VEIN OF GOLD—Elaine Camp
Houston had the land, and Faith had the skill. They were an unlikely team, but side by side they drilled the Texas soil for oil and found riches within each other.

SUMMER WINE—Freda Vasilos
The romance of Greece drew Sara into Nick's arms, but when the spell was broken she knew she could never leave her life in Boston for this alluring man . . . or could she?

DREAM GIRL—Tracy Sinclair
For an internationally known model like Angelique Archer, having a secret admirer was not that unusual, but finding out he was royalty was definitely not an everyday occurrence!

SECOND NATURE—Nora Roberts
Lenore was the first reporter to get the opportunity to interview best-selling author Hunter Brown. On a camping trip in Arizona she learned more about Hunter and herself than she'd bargained for.

AVAILABLE NOW:

STATE SECRETS
Linda Lael Miller

DATELINE: WASHINGTON
Patti Beckman

ASHES OF THE PAST
Monica Barrie

STRING OF PEARLS
Natalie Bishop

LOVE'S PERFECT ISLAND
Rebecca Swan

DEVIL'S GAMBIT
Lisa Jackson